# KNOT A
*Chance*

## DOMS OF THE COVENANT BOOK 3

# SAMANTHA COLE

***Knot a Chance***
Copyright ©2020 Samantha A. Cole
All Rights Reserved.
Published by Suspenseful Seduction Publishing.

Editing by Eve Arroyo—www.evearroyo.com

*Knot a Chance* is a work of fiction. Names, characters, businesses, organizations, places, events, and incidents either are the product of the author's imagination or are used fictitiously. Any resemblance to actual persons, living or dead, events, or locales is entirely coincidental.
No part of this book may be reproduced or used in any manner without the express written permission of the publisher except for the use of brief quotations in a book review. This ebook is licensed for your personal enjoyment only. This book may not be re-sold or given away to other people. If you would like to share this ebook with another person, please purchase an additional copy for each recipient. If you're reading this book and did not purchase it, or it was not purchased for your use only, then please return to your favorite ebook retailer and purchase your own copy. Thank you for respecting the hard work of this author.

# Author's Note

The story within these pages is completely fictional but the concepts of BDSM are real. If you do choose to participate in the BDSM lifestyle, please research it carefully and take all precautions to protect yourself. Fiction is based on real life but real life is *not* based on fiction. Remember—Safe, Sane and Consensual!

Any information regarding persons or places has been used with creative literary license so there may be discrepancies between fiction and reality. The missions and personal qualities of members of the military and law enforcement within have been created to enhance the story and, again, may be exaggerated and not coincide with reality.

The author has full respect for the members of the United States military and the varied members of law enforcement and thanks them for their continuing service in making this country as safe and free as possible.

# Who's Who and the History of Trident Security and the Covenant

***While not every character is in every book, these are the ones with the most mentions throughout the series. This guide will help keep readers straight about who's who.

Trident Security (TS) is a private investigative and military agency, co-owned by Ian and Devon Sawyer. With governmental and civilian contracts, the company got its start when the brothers and a few of their teammates from SEAL Team Four retired to the private sector. The original six-man team is referred to as the Sexy Six-Pack, as they were dubbed by Kristen Sawyer, née Anders, or the Alpha Team. They, along with Ian and Devon's brother, Nick, are now shareholders in the business. Trident had since expanded and former members of the military and law enforcement have been added to the staff. The company is located on a guarded compound, which was a former import/export company cover for a drug trafficking operation in Tampa, Florida. Three warehouses on the property were converted into large apartments, the TS offices, gym, and bunk rooms. There is also an obstacle course, a Main

Street shooting gallery, a helicopter pad, and more features necessary for training and missions.

In addition to the security business, there is a fourth warehouse that now houses an elite BDSM club, co-owned by Devon, Ian, and their cousin, Mitch Sawyer, who is the manager. A lot of time and money has gone into making The Covenant the most sought after membership in the Tampa/St. Petersburg area and beyond. Members are thoroughly vetted before being granted access to the elegant club.

There are currently over fifty Doms who have been appointed Dungeon Masters (DMs), and they rotate two or three shifts each throughout the month. At least four DMs are on duty at all times at various posts in the pit, playrooms, and the new garden, with an additional one roaming around. Their job is to ensure the safety of all the submissives in the club. They step in if a sub uses their safeword and the Dom in the scene doesn't hear or heed it, and make sure the equipment used in scenes isn't harming the subs.

The Covenant's security team takes care of everything else that isn't scene-related, and provides safety for all members and are essentially the bouncers. With the recent addition of the garden, and more private, themed rooms, the owners have expanded their self-imposed limit of 350 members. The fire marshal had approved them for 500 when the warehouse-turned-kink club first opened, but the cousins had intentionally kept that number down to maintain an elite status. Now with more room, they are increasing the membership to 500, still under the new maximum occupancy of 720.

Between Trident Security and The Covenant there's plenty of romance, suspense, and steamy encounters. Come meet the Sexy Six-Pack, their friends, family, and teammates.

## The Sexy Six-Pack (Alpha Team) and Their Significant Others

- Ian "Boss-man" Sawyer: Devon and Nick's brother; retired Navy SEAL; co-owner of Trident Security and The Covenant; husband/Dom of Angelina (Angel); father of Peyton Marie.
- Devon "Devil Dog" Sawyer: Ian and Nick's brother; retired Navy SEAL; co-owner of Trident Security and The Covenant; husband/Dom of Kristen; father of John Devon "JD."
- Ben "Boomer" Michaelson: retired Navy SEAL; explosives and ordnance specialist; husband/Dom of Katerina; son of Rick and Eileen.
- Jake "Reverend" Donovan: retired Navy SEAL; temporarily assigned to run the West Coast team; sniper; husband/Dom of Nick; brother of Mike; Whip Master at The Covenant.
- Brody "Egghead" Evans: retired Navy SEAL; computer specialist; husband/Dom of Fancy.
- Marco "Polo" DeAngelis: retired Navy SEAL; communications specialist and back up helicopter pilot; husband/Dom of Harper; father to Mara.
- Nick "Junior" Donovan (nee Sawyer): Ian and Devon's brother; current Navy SEAL; husband/submissive of Jake.
- Kristen "Ninja-girl" Sawyer: author of romance/suspense novels; wife/submissive of Devon; mother of "JD."
- Angelina "Angie/Angel" Sawyer: graphic artist; wife/submissive of Ian; mother of Peyton Marie.
- Katerina "Kat" Michaelson: dog trainer for law enforcement and private agencies; wife/submissive of Boomer.
- Millicent "Harper" DeAngelis: lawyer; wife/submissive of Marco; mother of Mara.

- Francine "Fancy" Maguire: baker; wife/submissive of Brody.

### Extended Family, Friends, and Associates of the Sexy Six-Pack

- Mitch Sawyer: Cousin of Ian, Devon, and Nick; co-owner/manager of The Covenant, Dom to Tyler and Tori.
- T. Carter: US spy and assassin; works for covert agency Deimos; Dom of Jordyn.
- Jordyn Alvarez: US spy and assassin; member of covert agency Deimos; submissive of Carter.
- Tyler Ellis: Stockbroker; lifestyle switch—Dom of Tori; submissive of Mitch.
- Tori Freyja: K9 trainer for veterans in need of assistance/service dogs; submissive of Mitch and Tyler.
- Parker Christiansen: owner of New Horizons Construction; husband/Dom of Shelby; adoptive father of Franco and Victor.
- Shelby Christiansen: stay-at-home mom; two-time cancer survivor; wife/submissive of Parker; adoptive mother of Franco and Victor.
- Curt Bannerman: retired Navy SEAL; owner of Halo Customs, a motorcycle repair and detail shop; husband of Dana; stepfather of Ryan, Taylor, Justin, and Amanda. Lives in Iowa.
- Dana Prichard-Bannerman: teacher; widow of retired SEAL Eric Prichard; wife of Curt; mother of Ryan, Taylor, Justin, and Amanda. Lives in Iowa.
- Jenn "Baby-girl" Mullins: college student; goddaughter of Ian; "niece" of Devon, Brody,

Jake, Boomer, and Marco; father was a Navy SEAL; parents murdered.
- Mike Donovan: owner of the Irish pub, Donovan's; brother of Jake; submissive to Charlotte.
- Charlotte "Mistress China" Roth: Parole officer; Domme and Whip Master at The Covenant; Domme of Mike.
- Travis "Tiny" Daultry: former professional football player; head of security at The Covenant and Trident compound; occasional bodyguard for TS.
- Doug "Bullseye" Henderson: retired Marine; head of the Personal Protection Division of TS.
- Rick and Eileen Michaelson: Boomer's parents; guardians of Alyssa. Rick is a retired Navy SEAL.
- Charles "Chuck" and Marie Sawyer: Ian, Devon, and Nick's parents. Charles is a self-made real estate billionaire. Marie is a plastic surgeon involved with Operation Smile.
- Will Anders: Assistant Curator of the Tampa Museum of Art Kristen Anders's cousin.
- Dr. Roxanne London: pediatrician; Domme/wife (Mistress Roxy) of Kayla; Whip Master at Covenant.
- Kayla London: social worker; submissive/wife of Roxanne.
- Grayson and Remington Mann: twins; owners of Black Diamond Records; Doms/fiancés of Abigail; members of The Covenant.
- Abigail Turner: personal assistant at Black Diamond Records; submissive/fiancée of Gray and Remi.

- Chase Dixon: retired Marine Raider; owner of Blackhawk Security; associate of TS.
- Reggie Helm: lawyer for TS and The Covenant; Dom/husband of Colleen.
- Alyssa Wagner: teenager saved by Jake from an abusive father; lives with Rick and Eileen Michaelson; attending nursing school.
- Dr. Trudy Dunbar: Psychologist.
- Carl Talbot: college professor; Dom and Whip Master at The Covenant.
- Jase Atwood: Contract agent/mercenary; Lives on the island of St. Lucia; Dom of Brie.
- Brie Hanson: Owner of Daddy-O's in St. Lucia; submissive of Jase.
- Stefan Lundquist: Lieutenant Commander US Coast Guard; Dom; Shibari Master.
- Cassandra Myers: Cardiac Rehabilitation Technician; attending nursing school; submissive.

## The Omega Team and Their Significant Others

- Cain "Shades" Foster: retired Secret Service agent.
- Tristan "Duracell" McCabe: retired Army Special Forces.
- Logan "Cowboy" Reese: retired Marine Special Forces; former prisoner of war. Boyfriend/Dom of Dakota.
- Valentino "Romeo" Mancini: retired Army Special Forces; former FBI Hostage Rescue Team (HRT) member.
- Darius "Batman" Knight: retired Navy SEAL.
- Kip "Skipper" Morrison: retired Army; former LAPD SWAT sniper.

- Lindsey "Costello" Abbott: retired Marine; sniper.
- Dakota Swift: Tampa PD undercover police officer; submissive girlfriend to Logan.
- Tahira: Princess of Timasur; wife of Darius.

## Trident Support Staff

- Colleen McKinley-Helm: office manager of TS; wife/submissive of Reggie.
- Tempest "Babs" Van Buren: retired Air Force helicopter pilot; TS mechanic.
- Russell Adams: retired Navy; assistant TS mechanic.
- Nathan Cook: former computer specialist with the National Security Agency (NSA).

## Members of Law Enforcement

- Larry Keon: Assistant Director of the FBI.
- Frank Stonewall: Special Agent in Charge of the Tampa FBI.
- Calvin Watts: Leader of the FBI HRT in Tampa.
- Colt Parrish: Major Case Specialist, Behavioral Analysis Unit.

## The K9s of Trident

- Beau: An orphaned Lab/Pit mix, rescued by Ian. Now a trained K9 who has more than earned his spot on the Alpha Team.
- Spanky: A rescued Bullmastiff with a heart of gold, owned by Parker and Shelby.
- Jagger: A rescued Rottweiler trained as an assistance/service animal for Russell.

- FUBAR: A Belgian Malinois who failed aggressive guard dog training. Adopted by Babs.
- BDSM: Bravo, Delta, Sierra, and Mike, two Belgian Malinoises and two German shepherds, the guard dogs at the Trident compound: Ian named them using the military communication's alphabet.

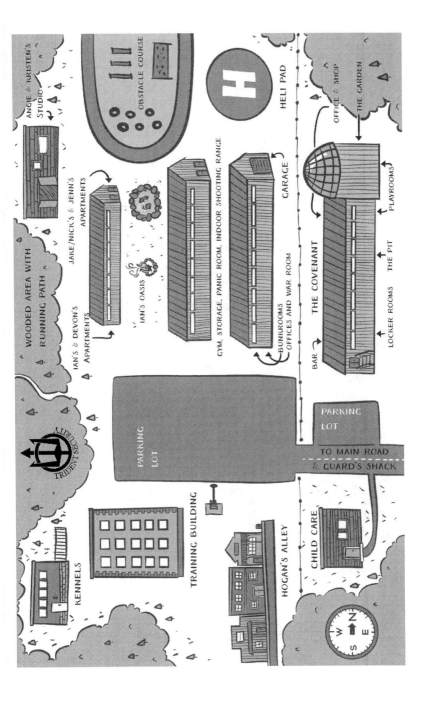

# ONE

"Red."

Stefan Lundquist's hand froze at the whispered word. The pen he was holding was an inch away from the contract he'd been about to sign, renewing his Dominant/submissive relationship with Cassandra Myers for another month. His brow furrowed as he was unsure he'd heard her correctly. "What did you say, Cassie?"

There was a long moment of silence as they sat across from each other at his dining room table. Stefan had invited her over to sign the contract, have some dinner, then play for a while, and she'd arrived only a few minutes ago. After the contract was out of the way and they'd eaten, he'd planned on trying a new Shibari design on the beautiful submissive's naked body before burying himself deep inside her. But if she'd said what he thought she'd just said, then none of that would happen.

He darkened his tone. "I expect an answer, Cassandra. Look at me and repeat yourself."

The twenty-nine-year-old blonde swallowed hard before her eyelids lifted and her gaze met his. Stefan's gut clenched when he saw her hazel eyes were filled with unshed tears.

Cassandra's voice was barely any louder when she spoke again. "I said, 'red,' Sir."

Stefan had no idea what was going on. They'd been in a D/s relationship for ten months now. On the ninth of each month, they'd sat down and discussed any changes either wanted to make to their contract before signing it for another four weeks. He'd thought tonight would be no different, but Cassandra obviously disagreed.

Dropping the pen atop the papers in front of him, he leaned back in his chair, crossed his arms, and stared at the sub. She was what Stefan's father would call "a stunner." Her long, blonde locks fell just below her shoulder blades, and he had to put them in a ponytail before he tied her up when they played so they were out of his way. A smattering of freckles dusted her nose and cheeks. Her bow-shaped lips were made to be kissed, and there were moments in the past when he'd completely lost track of time while exploring her mouth with his own.

The neckline of her shirt was wide and curved, exposing the porcelain skin of her shoulders and neck. As for the rest of her body, the woman had curves that gave most men whiplash as she sashayed past them. At five feet five, she was eight inches shorter than him unless she wore one of the several pairs of fuck-me heels she owned. Stefan loved when she wore them with nothing else on but his collar and ropes. Unfortunately, it appeared he wouldn't be seeing her dressed like that in the future.

"Why are you saying your safeword, little pixie? And, please, speak up."

She cleared her throat and straightened her back. Her voice was stronger this time but still worrisome. "I-I'm sorry, Sir, but I don't want to renew our contract this month."

Her lip trembled, and Stefan tried to figure out why. Was she scared of what he was going to do or say? He'd never given her a reason to be afraid of him. Was she nervous for some other reason? Or was she about to lie to him?

"I-I've had a lot of fun these past few months, but—but I'd rather not be collared by you or anyone else for a while, Sir."

Her gaze dropped to the table, and Stefan ground his teeth together, trying to keep his frustration in check. *Damn it.* Things had been going great with her. She was the most responsive sub he'd had in a long time when it came to Shibari. She loved being wrapped in his rope designs. The less she could move, the more explosive her orgasms were when he finally allowed her to come. What had changed?

They'd both gone into the relationship with a clear understanding. Each contract lasted exactly one month. They played either in his townhouse or at The Covenant, the elite BDSM club in Tampa they both belonged to. Cassandra waitressed there three evenings a week, four hours per shift, earning her a dramatic reduction in her membership fees in addition to tips. He knew that after living expenses, there wasn't much left over in her pay from her full-time career as a cardiac rehabilitation technician, so the extra job helped her financially and gave her access to the club.

"Cassie, eyes on me." An experienced sub, her response to his command was instantaneous. "You're my submissive until midnight tonight. Until I give you leave, you *will* follow protocol. Now, why don't you want to be collared anymore?"

She took a deep breath and let it out slowly, but her gaze stayed on his. "I've decided to go back to school, Sir, for nursing, and I won't have time for anything else between classes and work."

Okay, this wasn't as bad as he'd thought it was. As her Dom, he could help her. Stefan had recently been promoted to the rank of lieutenant commander in the Coast Guard. While military pay wasn't the greatest, the truth was, he didn't need it. His family came from old money, and a trust fund, which he rarely touched, had been set up for him by his grandfather shortly after Stefan had been born. None of his friends or fellow club members knew about his family's wealth, except The Covenant's three owners, Ian and Devon Sawyer, and their cousin Mitch. Their security guru, Brody Evans, also knew since he'd done the extensive background check on Stefan during the application process. All members and employees of The Covenant were completely vetted to help maintain privacy and safety, so any skeletons in an applicant's closet were sure to be found.

Despite his family's money, Stefan had been drawn to the military from a young age, although he couldn't recall what had originally set him on the path to enlisting. It was just something he'd always wanted to do. While his family had tried to encourage him to attend law school, like his older sister, Elin, Stefan had signed up for the Coast Guard following his college education, which allowed him to enlist as an officer.

Years vacationing in Martha's Vineyard had given him his love for the ocean, and the USCG had given him a better chance of serving on a ship or in a port while remaining in the US. At the time, that'd been important to him. Stefan had always been close to his maternal grandparents, and his greatest fear had been not being stationed near enough to get to them quickly if something happened to either of them. His grandmother had passed away nine years ago, but he'd been stationed in New Jersey and able to get to the hospital in time to say goodbye to her. Unfortunately, without any warning, his grandfather died of a heart attack four years later. While Stefan hadn't seen him before he passed, he'd been able to attend the funeral without the huge hassle of traveling from somewhere on the other side of the world.

Stefan ran a hand over his salt-and-pepper crewcut. Like

his father before him, he'd started going gray five years ago at the age of thirty-three. He didn't mind, though, because if he let his hair grow out, it was still thick and didn't recede at all. Quite a few friends from high school had already gone partially or completely bald, and he was glad he wasn't one of them. Not that he was vain. He just knew what he looked like completely bald after he and most of the men at The Covenant had shaved their heads in support of a pretty sub named Shelby when she'd been going through chemo. Thankfully, she'd beaten her cancer, but it'd been pretty funny to see all those polished heads before everyone's hair had started growing back.

Sighing, he pushed away all thoughts that didn't have to do with the current situation. To make certain they were both on the same page, he repeated some of Cassandra's words back to her. "So, between school and working at both the hospital and The Covenant, you won't have time to relax and play?"

"No, Sir."

While studying her face, he got the impression she wanted to bolt. He'd never seen her this nervous before and tried to soften his expression and tone of voice. "What if I took care of your membership fees? Then you'd be able to give up your job at The Covenant. Once you get your class schedule, we can plan playtime around it."

Her eyes had gone wide at his offer, but she'd started shaking her head before he'd finished speaking. "No—no, Sir. I-I can't let you do that. I'm sorry, but I think it's best that you take your collar back. There are plenty of unattached subs at the club. Several of them have already expressed interest in taking my place."

Stefan frowned. "You discussed this with the other subs before coming here tonight? Before telling me you want to be uncollared?" Hell, no, he was not happy about that. He should have been the first person to know she would use her safeword and return his collar, not the last. "You know better than that, subbie. Your discussing any part of our contract, or the termination of it, with anyone else is not acceptable."

"I'm s-sorry, Sir." Her tears welled up again. "I-I just thought it would be easier if I had a replacement ready for you—you need a sub for your Shibari classes."

That was true. In a few weeks, Stefan was set to begin teaching another course at the club in the fine art of tying a submissive up in designs made from yards of silky rope. When his maternal grandfather had taught Stefan how to create dozens of different types of knots when he was a boy, he never thought he'd be using the knowledge to decorate naked women with intricate patterns that would put them in subspace.

But Stefan didn't want a new sub—he wanted Cassandra. He'd gotten used to her, and they'd fallen into a comfortable relationship—superficial as it was. He'd made it clear when they'd done their initial negotiations all those months ago that they were a Dom and his sub—nothing more. Stefan didn't want a girlfriend or slave. He'd gone both those routes before—several times—and none had worked out, which was why he avoided those types of relationships now. Less drama that way.

Damn it, he wasn't ready to give Cassandra up yet. But he didn't have a choice. She'd said her safeword, and as a respectable Dom, he had to abide by it. That didn't mean he couldn't try to get her to change her mind. "We have a few hours left on the current contract. Do you still want to play tonight?"

When she hesitated and bit her bottom lip, his heart sank. He knew without a doubt what her next words were going to be. "No, Sir, I'd rather not. I'm sorry—I know you didn't expect this tonight, but I-I really should be going."

He had half a mind to ask where she was going in such a hurry but managed to keep the question in his throat. He didn't want her to know how disappointed he was that she'd ended their time together. Instead, he stood and rounded the table to stand behind her.

"Lift your hair," he commanded. When she obeyed him, his fingers went to her nape, but then he couldn't help himself. Before he unclasped the simple collar he'd given her months ago, he skimmed her bare neck and shoulder with his knuckles, memorizing how soft she was. A shiver flowed through her, and goosebumps appeared across her skin. Damn, he was going to miss her.

Taking a deep breath, he undid the clasp and removed the black leather and silver collar from her neck before stuffing it into the front pocket of his navy-blue Dockers. He wanted nothing more than to bend down and kiss his way across her shoulder to her neck and then nuzzle her ear. But if he did that, he'd be left standing there with a hard-on when she walked out the door.

Taking a step to the side, he held out his hand. When she took it, he helped her to her feet, then kissed the back of her hand. "It was an honor to be your Dom, Cassie. I wish you all the best." He couldn't resist adding, "As for my offer—paying your membership while you're in school—I'd like you to agree to it, no strings attached. This way, you only have to work one job and can better concentrate on your studies."

When it looked like she would turn him down again, he squeezed her hand. "Please accept my gift. It would mean a lot to me."

She sucked her bottom lip between her teeth. Seconds ticked by as she held his brown-eyed gaze before nodding. "If it means that much to you, Sir, thank you."

He knew the smile on his face didn't reach his eyes, but he tried to keep the tone of his voice light. "No, thank *you*, Cassie. It's my pleasure. Maybe it'll give us the opportunity to play on occasion."

It didn't escape his notice that she winced slightly at his hopeful statement. He wanted to ask her about it but thought it was best not to. He'd find out soon, but not tonight. She was too upset, and he got the feeling she'd shut down further if he interrogated her. He'd figured out months ago the best way to get Cassandra to open up was to tie her down. And that clearly wasn't going to happen right now. "I'll talk to Master Mitch tomorrow and make the arrangements. He'll probably need two weeks' notice."

"That's fine, Sir. Classes start next Wednesday, so they'll only overlap with my club shift for a few days—I've already arranged for two of my shifts to be covered by other waitresses." When he didn't release her hand, she glanced down to where they were joined. "I-I really should go."

With great reluctance, Stefan let her go and then escorted her to the front door, where he fought the urge to kiss her. "Goodbye, little pixie."

"Goodbye, Sir."

Ten minutes after she walked out of his life, Stefan sat on his living room couch with an almost empty glass of scotch—one that had been filled for the second time moments before. He stared at the coiled lengths of rope he'd set out on the coffee table earlier in the evening. There was a new design he'd wanted to try out on her tonight. With the aid of two hooks in the ceiling, the pattern would have looked like Cassie had wings when he was done with it—like a heavenly angel. But now all he had were the memories of their past time together—for once in his life, he didn't think it was enough.

# Two

Cassandra managed to hold off her tears until she climbed into her car and slammed the door shut. Once she had her privacy, fat, wet drops rolled down her cheeks. Tonight was one of the worst nights of her life. The last thing she'd ever wanted to do was have Sir remove her collar, but she couldn't continue with their relationship as it had been.

Opening the center console between the bucket seats, she retrieved a package of tissues and pulled several of them out. As she blew her nose, she looked out her windshield. She'd parked in one of the complex's spots reserved for visitors, directly across the street from Stefan's bi-level townhouse. The blinds to the living room in his unit were closed. She'd half expected him to watch her leave and wasn't sure if she was relieved or disappointed he hadn't. The fact he hadn't told her she'd made the right decision tonight. She'd been just another sub to him, while she'd wanted to be so much more than that.

She was about to start the engine of her Corolla when her phone chimed a text. With shaking hands, she pulled her cell from her purse and checked the screen. The message was from her friend and coworker at The Covenant, Sasha Lewis.

SASHA

Did you leave yet? How did it go?

Taking a shuddering breath, Cass typed in her response.

Not well. Can I come over?

SASHA

Of course! I'll break out a bottle of wine and some Twinkies

Twenty minutes later, Cass lifted her hand to knock on the door to Sasha's apartment, but it swung open before she could. Her full-figured friend pulled her into a big, warm embrace. "Girlfriend, I'm so sorry. Men can suck moose shit sometimes—even Doms. Get in here and have a drink."

Cass followed her inside and shut the door behind them. As soon as she deposited her purse on one of the kitchen chairs, Sasha thrust a full glass of Pinot Grigio into her hand. She then clinked her own glass against Cass's. "Subbies unite!"

After they both sipped the sweet white wine, Sasha linked her arm with Cass's and steered her toward the couch. "Now, sit and tell me what happened. What did you say? What did he say? Was he mad? Please tell me you didn't cry in front of him. I can't see Master Stefan letting you leave if you were crying."

That was true. He definitely wouldn't have let her go in tears, which is why she'd done her best to get out of there before shedding a single one.

Sighing, she sat beside her friend and wasn't surprised when Flash, Sasha's cat, ran over and jumped into her lap for some loving. He was mostly black with a white streak across one eye and ear. Absentmindedly, Cass stroked the animal's soft fur while she spoke. "I told Sir I couldn't manage to work both jobs, go back to school, and be his sub all at the same time. He wasn't happy, but he let me out of the contract.'

"Just like that?" Sasha's tone said she knew Cass was leaving a lot out. "Girl, don't make me get you drunk to get the rest of it. Now, talk."

She took a large gulp of wine before answering. "He wants to pay for my club membership so I don't have to work there while going to school." Sasha's eyes bulged, and Cass shrugged. "He refused to take no for an answer."

"He's paying your membership? With no strings attached?"

"Yeah, do you believe that? I mean, it's a lot of money." Membership to The Covenant, one of the most elite BDSM clubs on the Gulf Coast of Florida, wasn't cheap. "He said maybe we could play sometimes, but it wasn't necessary for letting him pay my dues. He said it was a gift."

Sasha huffed. "Well, that's good. Otherwise, it would be like you were his call girl or something."

Cass hadn't thought of it that way, but her friend was right. If play and sex had been a requirement, she never would've agreed to the arrangement. She'd had a hard-enough time consenting to it in the first place.

"I just don't get Doms sometimes," the other sub continued. "I mean, you two were great together—you were just like every other happy couple in the place, so why wouldn't Stefan sign a longer contract with you?"

A fresh tear rolled down Cass's cheek. "Because he means more to me than I will ever mean to him. He told me from the get-go that the contract would be month to month and our relationship wouldn't go further than a simple D/s one. I was just stupid enough to go and fall in love with him."

Sasha reached over and patted Cass's knee. "You weren't stupid, girlfriend. Shit like this happens all the time. You can't help it if you fell for a dumb-ass Dom. But you'll get past it, and somewhere out there is a Dom who will deserve your love."

The problem was Cass couldn't see herself falling for anyone other than the one man who didn't want her love. For the first time since a few months after she'd joined The Covenant, she was afraid of the prospect of having to find a new Dom.

# THREE

*Five years earlier...*

Ian Sawyer eyed The Covenant's new waitress, Cassandra. She was dressed in the outfit all the club's female employees wore—a black bra and pleated mini-skirt, with a red and gold bow tie. On her feet were a simple pair of black, ballet-type slippers. She was nice, cute, and good at her job, but he was worried about her. She'd been working there for eleven weeks, and aside from the required basic classes for submissives, she'd yet to play with any of the available Doms. He knew several had approached her to negotiate a scene, but she'd politely yet effectively turned them down.

Ian had given her time to settle in, but as the Dom-in-residence, it was up to him to figure out what was going on with the blonde sub. While he co-owned the club with his brother Devon and their cousin, Mitch, who also managed the place, Ian was more experienced and trained in the lifestyle than the other two men. Yesterday, Mitch had asked him to talk to Cassandra since she didn't have to interact with Ian as an employee on a regular basis. They didn't want her to feel her job was jeopardized if she wasn't willing to play. However, from her initial interview for the cocktail waitress position and her questions in the submissive's class, they knew she was interested in exploring the lifestyle. Still, she didn't seem to have the courage to take that final step. Ian would try to change that tonight.

He watched as she dropped off a few drinks to two Masters and their subs, who were sitting in one of the lounging areas near the bar on the balcony level of the BDSM club. Before she could take any other orders, Ian strode over to intercept her. "Cassandra."

Her eyes dilated at his deep, rumbling voice as he approached, then her gaze dropped to the floor in submission. "Yes, Master Ian?"

"Please leave your tray at the bar, then meet me in playroom number four."

"W-what, S-Sir?" Forgetting protocol, she now stared at him in confusion. "I don't—"

His tone left no room for an argument. "That wasn't a request, subbie. I'll be there in five minutes and expect you to be in a perfect present position when I arrive."

"Y-yes, Sir."

He could hear the fear in her voice but didn't address it at the moment. Ian wanted her off guard for their conversation —he'd found that when submissives were keeping something inside, emotionally, they tended to be more forthcoming with the truth about what was bothering them if they were caught by surprise.

As she hurried to the waitress station at one end of the bar, with a few wary glances over her shoulder at him, Ian moved to the opposite end where Master Brody was drawing a draft beer. The club's regular Wednesday night bartender was at the ER, getting his hand stitched up after slicing it with a piece of broken glass ten minutes after starting his shift earlier, so Trident Security's computer geek was filling in.

Brody eyed him. "What's up?"

"I'm taking Cassandra off-duty early. Kimmy and Miranda can handle things now that people have started heading out."

Setting the glass of Guinness in front of the Dom who'd ordered it, Brody made certain no one else needed his attention before asking, "You gonna try to get in her head?"

When Ian nodded, his friend continued. "She's a sweet thing, hot as sin too, but something is definitely bugging her. I mean, she's turned me down a bunch of times, with and without Marco joining us. What submissive does that?"

"A smart one with taste."

With a snort and a chuckle, Brody shook his head and stepped over to where he was being flagged for another drink. "Keep it up, Boss-man. Just remember, I have access to all your passwords. The next time someone calls you, don't be surprised if you have a new ringtone."

Ian wouldn't put it past the guy, who was lucky his bosses and teammates at Trident Security knew his worth. They couldn't kill him but would definitely find new ways to make him suffer. Of course, that would only result in some retaliation, but that was nothing new.

Putting those thoughts aside, Ian headed for the grand staircase that led into the pit. A burly security guard stood sentry, holding a device that checked members' ID cards. Alcoholic drinks ordered at the bar or through one of the waitresses were put on the members' cards, which were then scanned before entry to the scene areas was allowed. There was a two-drink maximum for anyone wishing to play, but most members preferred not to drink at all until after they were done scening for the night.

Ian didn't have a card to be scanned. The three owners had written the club rules together and practiced how they preached. He'd only enjoyed two ounces of his favorite whiskey over ninety minutes ago, so he was still in the right frame of mind to mess with the submissive—something he loved to do. The psychological games of the BDSM lifestyle could be just as fun and satisfying as the physical ones.

Dipping his chin once at the guard as he passed, Ian descended the stairs and greeted a few members along the way. After crossing over to the other side of the pit, he veered toward the hallway on the left, where Playroom #4 was located. Marco DeAngelis, another one of his employees and teammates at Trident, was on dungeon monitor duty, stationed at the entrance to the hallway, and Ian stopped next to him. "Do me a favor and stand outside four. I want Cassandra to be assured that if she yells her safeword, you'll step in and stop the scene. I'll have her yell 'red' before I start. Just stick your head in."

"No problem. You going to mind-fuck her and find out what she's hiding behind?"

"Yeah. She's had plenty of time to get comfortable and should've been playing by now. I think she wants to, but something's holding her back. She's scared to scene, for whatever reason, and unless we drag it out of her, she'll never move forward." Ian walked down the hallway to the closed door of Playroom #4 with Marco beside him.

"Think she was abused?"

"Not sure, but I wouldn't be surprised to find out someone's fucked with her head, at the very least. I've seen her watching scenes, and you can tell she's positively affected by most of them, but then she turns down every Dom who approaches her. It's time to find out what's going on in that mind of hers."

"I'll be waiting."

Ian nodded, then opened the door and stepped inside, closing it behind him again. Cassandra was kneeling on the floor, her head bowed, her ass on the heels of her feet, and her hands palms-up on her thighs. While her positioning wasn't perfect, it was pretty close. He walked around her, waiting to see if she'd look up at him, which she didn't. She was definitely a submissive and had the instincts of a good one, but that was only the start.

After a moment, he gently set his hand on the crown of her head and felt a shiver course through her. "Sit up straight, subbie."

She sat up a little higher, pushing her shoulders back, which thrust her breasts forward.

"Good girl."

The playroom contained several custom-made pieces of BDSM apparatus, implements used to inflict pain and/or pleasure, and several cabinets used to store anything a Dom might need during a scene. The one thing missing in this particular playroom was a bed, and it was one of the reasons Ian had selected it. While he hoped he'd be playing with the sub in a little while and coaxing an orgasm or two from her, he wouldn't be having sex with her at all. That wasn't the point of this session. He'd take care of himself later.

In one corner of the room, there was a comfortable red leather chair, and he pulled it over, placing it right in front of Cassandra. He removed several folded papers from the back pocket of his brown leathers, then took a seat, setting one boot-covered ankle on top of the opposite knee. "Now, it's time we had a little talk, subbie. Eyes on me."

---

Cassandra gulped, slowly lifting her chin until her gaze met Master Ian's. Her heart pounded as fear coursed through her —not of him, exactly, but of the unknown. Ever since he'd ordered her to come to this playroom, she'd been racking her brain, trying to figure out what she'd done wrong. Was she going to be fired or otherwise punished for some reason? Either way, she was worried.

She knew from chatting with the club's submissives and other employees that Ian, Devon, and Mitch Sawyer were highly-respected Doms—meaning they would never harm a submissive physically, emotionally, or psychologically. Now, hurting a sub safely, sanely, and consensually was a different story. On many nights, she'd witnessed the three unattached club owners play with different submissives. In fact, it was often the submissives who requested to scene with the Doms. She'd observed public scenes where their submissives were begging for release and, when the Doms allowed it, screaming as their orgasms crashed over them. How Cassandra wished she could be one of them, but she was afraid it would never happen.

When she'd first heard about the waitstaff position at the year-old BDSM club through a friend of hers who was in the lifestyle, she'd been thrilled to learn it came with access to the club at a significant reduction in dues as a perk. She could work off her membership fee, still make some extra money, and explore the lifestyle to her content. So far, two out of three was all she'd managed. She'd gone through the basic submissive course, learning the protocols and simple types of play. She'd been spanked by a Dom-in-training, experienced some mild sensation play, and even had Master Marco demonstrate on her how to warm up a submissive's skin with a flogger in preparation for a more intense scene. But none of that had included any sexual play—in other words, no one had drawn a climax from her, not that she'd expected them to be able to.

At twenty-four years old, Cassandra had never had an orgasm before, and it wasn't for lack of trying. She'd had several boyfriends over the years and had been sexually active since the age of eighteen, but she'd never experienced what made a woman scream out her lover's name and have her body quake with sheer pleasure. She'd read numerous romance novels over the years, but that was as close to the big "O" as she'd ever gotten.

After her first two boyfriends had complained she was unresponsive during sex, just lying there, she'd learned how to fake it. She'd found some websites with romantic porn for women and studied their movements. She'd practiced in bed with her vibrator, which had always made her feel good but had never given her a real, mind-shattering orgasm. Her few boyfriends after that had apparently never known the difference when she bounced and squirmed and screamed their names at what seemed to be the appropriate time.

Six months ago, Cassandra had come across a new book by her favorite author, Kristen Anders. All the woman's previous books had been "vanilla"—a word Cassandra had been accustomed to in the romance genre—but this new one had centered around the BDSM lifestyle. She didn't know why, but she'd been drawn to it almost immediately. At first, she'd just thought it was a fantasy world—it had been fiction, after all—but during a conversation about the book with her friend Erica, Cassandra discovered the lifestyle was real.

Erica explained that she and her longtime boyfriend had been in a D/s relationship for three years. She'd given Cassandra the links to several websites to check out and taken her to a munch, where newbies and those interested in learning more about the lifestyle could get answers to their questions from experienced Doms and subs. It was there Cassandra had heard about the waitstaff position she now held. Between her research and time at the club, she'd learned a lot, but she was still afraid to venture into any play that would become an embarrassment when the Dom she was with found out she couldn't orgasm.

"From what Master Mitch told me, during your job interview, you expressed a desire to immerse yourself into the lifestyle. This is your limit list." He held up the familiar-looking papers and then scanned through them. "Nothing here too out of the ordinary. So, I'm curious why you haven't accepted any scenes the Doms have approached you with. I know there have been plenty who have asked, offering a wide variety of play, but you've turned them all down. I could see if you wanted to avoid the sadists or the baby Doms, but it seems that everyone in between is not to your liking either. According to your list, you're into men and not women, so it's not that the wrong gender has been approaching you. So . . ."

He let the pages fall to the floor beside him, then crossed his arms. "Tell me why you haven't played yet."

Cassandra's mouth was dry. She didn't know what to say but was worried if she didn't respond at all, she would be fired. "I-I don't know, Sir."

*Oh, yeah, that was a great answer, Cass. That won't get you in trouble at all. At least you're remembering to call him Sir.*

"Eyes on me, sub. Look away again without my permission, and there will be consequences."

She hadn't realized she was now staring at the toe of his one boot that remained on the floor, and she forced her gaze to return to his face. His chiseled jaw was covered with a scruffy shadow that only added to his good looks. He and his brothers had gotten their black hair and piercing blue eyes from their Irish ancestry. At six foot two and in his mid to late thirties, Master Ian was a wall of solid muscle, and it was easy to imagine him in his days as a Navy SEAL with his honed physique. He was usually a very nice boss—strict though—but right now, as he gave her a Dom scowl that'd caused many submissives to quake in their stocking feet, Cassandra shivered under his scrutiny. "I-I'm so-sorry, Sir. Please don't fire me."

Her eyes welled up, and she was embarrassed when the tears streaked down her face. She was reacting like a small child, and that wasn't a normal response for her. Outside the club, she was confident and determined, but once she crossed the threshold into The Covenant, that all changed.

She was surprised to see Master Ian's glare soften as he stood and placed both hands on her shoulders. "Breathe, little one. Take a deep breath and let it out. Do it now . . . good. Again."

His fingers tapped against her upper back, emphasizing his command. She complied, then licked the salty tears from her lips.

"Good, girl. And I can assure you, you're not being fired. I'm sorry if I gave you that impression." Sitting back down, he resumed his earlier position. "Now, I want you to yell your safeword—red."

Her still-wet eyes narrowed in confusion. "Sir?"

"Yell your safeword," he prompted.

She had no idea why he wanted her to say it but did as she was told. "Red."

Master Ian rolled his eyes and dropped his elevated foot to the floor with a resounding *thump*. "Louder, subbie."

"Red."

"Louder!" He leaned toward her, resting his forearms on his knees. "I'm doing something you don't want me to do, and you want everyone in the club to know it. Your safeword, yell it! Now!"

"Red!" she screamed.

The door to the hallway flew open, and there stood Master Marco, one of tonight's dungeon monitors. In addition to his black leather pants and boots, he wore a gold vest. His penetrating gaze zeroed in on her, clearly assessing the situation. "Are you okay, little subbie?"

Cassandra glanced back and forth between the two men, bewildered about what was going on. "I-I think so, S-Sir. I-I don't—"

Master Ian reached out and gently cupped her jaw, cutting off her words and bringing her attention back to him. "Master Marco will be outside the door the entire time you and I are in here. He's there for one reason and one reason only. If you scream your safeword during our time together, he will burst in here, like he just did, and everything stops. You will not be in trouble at all for using your safeword. Understood?"

"Y-yes . . . I mean, no, S-Sir." She inhaled deeply and then tried to express herself better. "I mean, yes, I understand if I yell my safeword, Master Marco will come back in, but I still don't understand why. I mean, why am I in here . . . with you?" She knew she was babbling but couldn't help it. She really had no clue what was happening.

Leaning back in the chair, Master Ian gave the other Dom a nod of his head. Master Marco stepped outside the door and shut it again.

Master Ian's gaze grew more intense as it pinned Cassandra in place. "Because unless you say your safeword, we're going to play, little subbie."

# Four

Cassandra gulped. "P-play?"

Master Ian ignored her question. "I assume you've had some sexual experiences before now, correct?"

She stiffened like a deer caught in headlights. *Really? Did he just ask if I'm a virgin, or am I imagining things?*

"I won't repeat myself, subbie. If you can't stay focused on my questions and provide me with prompt, intelligent answers, I'll start tallying up your offenses for punishment later."

*Oh, shit!* "Um, sorry, Sir. I was caught off guard." When he just raised his eyebrows and glared at her, she hurried to continue. "I'm not a virgin if that's what you're asking, Sir."

"Tell me about your experiences."

*What?* She shook her head. "Um, I'm sorry, but what exactly do you want to know, Sir?"

"You've had what? One long-term relationship, several boyfriends, a bunch of one-night stands, or a combination of all three?"

She fought the urge to look away from his intense gaze—

he was serious about those punishments. "A combination, I guess, but only one one-night stand. None of my relationships ever worked out."

"And why is that?"

Her shoulders hitched up to her ears. "I-I don't know, Sir. We just weren't compatible."

His head tilted as he studied her, and then his voice softened. "Were you ever sexually assaulted, Cassandra?"

"No, Sir." Her response had been immediate. Thankfully, that was one issue she'd never had to deal with, although she knew several women who'd endured the horror of being sexually assaulted or harassed.

"Good, I'm glad to hear that."

He paused, and the sudden silence in the room unsettled her. Several moments passed before he asked, "Have you ever had an orgasm, Cassandra?"

Oh, God, she didn't want to talk about that. It was so embarrassing. There she was, in a private room, dressed in a skimpy outfit, with a gorgeous Dom, and he wanted her to admit she'd never come in her life?

"Eyes on me, sub. That's five."

Her gaze flew to his. She hadn't even realized it'd shifted again until he'd mentioned it. Her lip quivered, and tears flowed down her cheeks again. She sniffled and inwardly cursed. All her life, she'd been an ugly crier, and she could only imagine what the Dom thought of her right now. "I-I'm sorry, Sir. I-I can't talk about this."

Instead of responding, Master Ian stood and strode over to one of the cabinets. When he returned, he had a dark red scarf in his hands. Stepping behind her, he placed the material over her eyes and tied the ends behind her head. She was startled when she felt him kneel behind her and straddle her calves. He grasped her shoulders and gently pulled until her back impacted his hard chest.

"Shh, little one." His low, sexy voice sent shivers down her spine. "Relax."

His hands caressed her arms down to her wrists and back up to her shoulders before repeating the motions. Goosebumps peppered her skin as it warmed under his touch. He pushed her long, blonde hair out of his way, and his lips found the soft column of her neck. He kissed his way upward. Cassandra inhaled sharply as a stirring started in her core. While it was something she'd felt many times before, nothing ever became of it. But this time, it was different. This time it was with a Dom who could do all the things she'd dreamed of if only she were bold enough to let him.

Master Ian's heated breath teased her ear. "There are no right or wrong answers to my questions, Cassandra. I'm trying to help you, but I can't do that if you refuse to answer me. Normally, I'd add to the punishment, but I don't think that's what you need. You're a beautiful woman, and any Dom would be lucky to win your heart. That Dom isn't me, but I'm willing to help you get past whatever it is that's holding you back. If we stay like this and talk, will you have the courage to answer me?"

With her sight gone, her other senses were on high alert. Her skin tingled with anticipation. What would Master Ian do next? She knew why he'd said he wasn't the Dom who would win her heart—many D/s relationships had nothing to do with love, and he didn't want her thinking he was offering more than he was willing to give. By not being able to see him, though, it was making it easier to talk to him. For some reason, her fear was ebbing—in fact, she was getting seriously turned on. "I-I think so, Sir."

"Good girl." He nipped her ear, and her clit began to throb in time with her elevated heart rate. "Now, I asked you a question earlier, subbie, and this time I expect a truthful answer. Have you ever had an orgasm?"

"Not really, Sir."

She felt him smile against her neck. "That means no. Your boyfriends were very selfish if they never took the time to pleasure you."

"Th-they tried, Sir. I don't think it was their fault. Most of them, at least. Some of them told me I was a cold fish in bed." He growled against her skin—clearly, he didn't like hearing that. "But maybe I am because I'm definitely not the wildcat they apparently wanted. I guess I'm just incapable of having orgasms."

"I highly doubt that's true, and I'd like the opportunity to prove you and them wrong. Will you let me?"

Would she? Part of her wanted to take him up on his offer, while the other part feared this would be her last chance to feel like a normal woman. If she failed to orgasm this time, she'd probably spend the rest of her life not knowing what it was like to fly into utter bliss. Should she turn over her mind and body to this sensual Dom whose tongue, lips, and teeth were currently grazing against her shoulder, making her want to beg for more? "I'm scared to, Sir."

"You may be scared, Cassandra, but you're also turned on. I can smell your intoxicating scent from here."

Well, damn, she'd been hoping he hadn't noticed that.

His hands ran slowly down her arms to her sides until they stopped at her hips. He clutched her flesh, digging his fingertips into her. It didn't hurt, but instead, it made her feel restrained in a way. Her breathing increased, and a soft moan escaped her.

"Will you let me pleasure you? There will be no intercourse—I want nothing from you but the opportunity to make you come."

Damn, his words alone were bringing her closer to the edge. Could this work? Could she finally experience what the other female submissives had at the hands of their Doms? There was only one way to find out. "Yes, Sir."

"Yes, Sir, what?"

She licked her lips and swallowed hard. "Yes, Sir, please make me come."

His lips brushed against her temple. "It will be my honor. But tell me something first. What scenes turn you on the most when you're walking around the club?"

That was easy. "The ones where the submissives are restrained, Sir."

Her hair was moved from one shoulder to the other, and his mouth gave the newly exposed flesh the same treatment the other side had gotten. "That's a broad range. Have you ever been restrained to the point you couldn't move at all, and you were completely at someone's mercy?"

Nope, she hadn't been. She'd asked a few boyfriends she'd trusted to tie her up, but she'd never given them complete control over her—she could've easily gotten out of the scarves she'd had them use to restrain her wrists. In all her recent fantasies, however, she was tied down—legs, arms, and torso— to the point she couldn't move and had to take whatever her Dom gave her. Even now, the thought made her wetter than she'd been a few moments ago. Never had she come this close to begging a man to fuck her into oblivion, and all they'd done so far was just talk. "No, Sir."

"Is that a green for tonight's play? Restraining you until you can't move at all—until you can't stop me from doing whatever I want unless you say your safeword?" When she hesitated, he added, "Remember, Master Marco is still right outside that door. You're safe with me. If you yell red, I'll immediately stop and untie you, and then we'll talk about what went wrong. But if you don't, I'll do everything in my power to make you shatter under my touch."

Cassandra panted as her heart threatened to beat out of her chest. *Oh, God, I'm really going to do this!*

He'd left her no choice but to surrender her body, which was yearning for what he'd proposed. "Y-yes, Sir. I'd like that very much. And I'm okay with being restrained, Sir."

"Thank you for trusting me, Cassandra. I won't be doing anything to you tonight that's not on your green or yellow list, but if you're uncomfortable with something you thought you'd like to try, then say the word yellow. I'll slow down, and then we'll discuss it before moving forward. Understood?"

"Yes, Sir." The green levels of play are things she'd done before or wanted to do without reservations. The yellow ones were activities she was interested in but unsure whether she'd like them or not. Reds were things she had no desire to try.

He moved away from her, and from the sound of creaking leather, she assumed he'd risen. "Leave the scarf over your eyes and give me your hand." She lifted her arm until he grasped her hand. "Stand."

With his help, she got to her feet, and then he turned her until she was facing in the other direction. Without letting go of her hand, he said, "Take four steps forward."

Once she stopped, he set her hands on a leather-covered piece of equipment—it was probably the spanking bench she'd seen when she'd first walked into the room. A shiver ran down her spine.

"Strip, subbie, and place your clothing on the bench in front of you, neatly folded. Then present for me—feet shoulder-width apart and hands behind your head, elbows back. Leave the blindfold on."

Her hands shook—not from the embarrassment of undressing in front of Master Ian, but the fact the action would take her one step closer to hopefully achieving what she'd thought was impossible.

As she removed her skirt, bra, thong, slippers, and bowtie,

she heard him moving about the room, opening and closing several cabinets and drawers. After she was completely naked, and her clothes were folded in a pile in front of her, she spread her feet a little wider and clasped her hands together just above her nape.

"Good girl." He shuffled about the room, and around the edges of the silk scarf, she tried unsuccessfully to see what he was doing. "Take a step forward and climb on the bench."

Her clothes had been moved away. Master Ian's hands guided her until she was lying prone on top of the bench, her knees and elbows bent and resting on padded shelves. "Relax, little one."

"I'm trying to, Sir."

She heard the ripping of Velcro and felt him bind her right arm down just above her wrist. Seconds later, the same was done to her left. Both times, he slid his finger under the strap to make certain it wasn't too tight. She tugged on the restraints, testing them. While her circulation wasn't being cut off, she also couldn't pull her hands free. Next, her calves and thighs were bound in a similar fashion.

"Let me know if you feel any tingling or pain in your hands or feet."

"Yes, Sir. They feel fine."

Finally, two wider straps crossed over her upper and lower back. The only things she could move were her head, hands, and feet, and she could just wiggle her hips a fraction in all directions. Instead of feeling trapped, Cassandra felt free. She couldn't explain it if she tried, but a sense of Zen flowed over her.

Master Ian's hand ran up her thigh and over the curve of her ass. She squirmed under his touch.

*Smack!* His hand had come down hard on her butt cheek.

"Ouch!" It'd stung, but her response had been more from the unexpected slap and sound than the actual pain.

He growled softly. "Quiet, subbie. From here on, the only words I want to hear from your pretty mouth are 'yes, Sir' and 'no, Sir' if I ask you a question or your safewords. Do not move your hips at all. Understood?"

"Yes, Sir."

His hand resumed its gentle grazing up her back, past her scapulas. The parts of her skin that were exposed rejoiced at his touch. He surprised her when he kneaded her shoulders and neck like a masseur. "Relax, Cassandra. Take a deep breath and let it out slowly . . . good. Again."

As she started to feel as if she were floating, he rolled something sharp along her upper arm, over her shoulder, and down the exposed areas of her back. Her mind warred with the pleasure/pain she was experiencing. It hurt, but it didn't.

"This is a Wartenberg wheel—it's used in sensation play." The pointy pins rolled over her ass cheek and down her thigh to her knee before going up the other leg. "Are you still green, subbie?"

"Y-yes, Sir." She was more than green.

As the wheel rolled up the opposite side of her torso, Master Ian's other hand dropped between her legs. She gasped when his fingers brushed against her sex. The fact that she couldn't stop what he was doing to her by pulling away turned her on even more.

"Mmm. You're getting nice and wet for me. That's a good start, but you'll be dripping soon."

He ran his fingers through her folds before moving further to her clit. The little nub was already swollen, and she couldn't help it when she bucked her hips—not that they got far. She almost cried out when his hand and the wheel left her body.

"That's five more, subbie."

Before she had a chance to think about his words, his hand lit up her backside. Each strike landed on a different area on her ass cheeks and sit spots. After every other one, he held his hand against her skin, and she felt the heat infuse her flesh and spread. The pain was exquisite—something she'd never experienced before in her life.

When he reached ten, he didn't pause before plunging his fingers into her pussy. He'd been right—she was now dripping for him. It was amazing the difference between her past lovers and this dominant man who clearly knew his way around a woman's body. Her body and mind didn't even have a chance to process what she wanted him to do next before he was already doing it.

"You were made to be fucked properly, subbie. Those wimps didn't take the time to read your body's reactions like I'm doing now. I can feel the walls of your cunt trembling with the need to release all that pent-up sexual frustration. It's coming soon, I promise."

His dirty words spun through her mind, and her panting grew harder. She could feel a tightness rising within her, waiting to burst.

She heard something snap and felt cool liquid drip between the crack of her still-burning ass cheeks. While two fingers fucked her pussy, a thumb rubbed her clit, and another finger played with her little asshole.

"Have you ever been taken back here, subbie?"

The thought of him fucking her ass scared and excited her at the same time. She gripped the padded arms of the bench, trying not to shift her hips away. He hadn't done anything to harm her, and she still had her safeword. But the need to explode under his touch was far greater than the urge to yell out the word red. From his tone, it was evident Master Ian knew what her answer would be, but as a good sub should, she responded anyway. "No, Sir."

"Relax your ass. I'm only going to use one finger—nothing more. I want to give the nerves in there a little taste of what it'll be like when either I or someone else takes you there.

With the right preparation, you'll fucking love it. But for now, just a little pressure. Are you ready for me to send you over the edge?"

Cassandra felt like she was being drawn up into a tornado. Her surroundings, body, and mind were spinning out of control. She couldn't hold back if she tried. This was it—the orgasm she'd been dreaming of. "Oh, God! Yes, Sir!"

"Then come for me." He simultaneously thrust into her, pressed down on her clit, and pushed his finger against the tight ring of her anus.

She exploded into a ball of heated passion, followed by wave after wave of pleasure coursing through her. She involuntarily screamed as his fingers drew out her climax, then sought to pull a second one from her body. Cassandra hadn't thought it was possible, but he managed to do just that. "That's a good girl—squirting all over my hand."

His words might've embarrassed her if she hadn't been floating on cloud nine. As her mind buzzed and she gasped for air, all her muscles went lax. The only reasons she didn't slide off the bench into a puddle of goo were the straps and Master Ian's hands, which slowed and then stopped.

As she descended back to Earth, he gently kissed the back of her head. "Welcome to The Covenant, subbie. I think you're ready to start playing with the other Doms, hmm?"

# FIVE

***Present...***

"Damn it! Where the fuck are they?" Using a pair of hi-tech binoculars, Stefan scanned the vast Gulf of Mexico from the open side door of a Coast Guard Search and Rescue (SAR) helicopter. His team was looking for four souls who'd been aboard a small plane that'd gone down over twenty minutes ago. Air traffic controllers at Tampa International Airport had intercepted the mayday call from the pilot less than a minute before the 2006 four-seater Cessna 172 Skyhawk had disappeared from the radar. It was reported that two young children and their parents had been onboard the plane.

Stefan hoped like hell they found them soon, but it was like looking for four eyelashes in a swimming pool. There hadn't been any signal from an emergency locator transmitter (ELT) so far. While all planes were required by the NTSB—National Transportation Safety Board—to have them, they weren't one hundred percent reliable. Sometimes, they failed to activate, and SAR crews were left struggling to find signs of life in the water like Stefan and his team were now. Several boats and aircraft were also on the way to the last known coordinates, but their helo had gotten there ahead of the rest.

Normally, as a lieutenant commander, Stefan wouldn't have been up in the air—his promotion last year usually had him running things from the Sector Command Center (SCC) at USCG Sector St. Petersburg now. He was a shift commander for the Incident Management Division, which directed and controlled the response to emergencies, including SAR coordination, pollution incidents, marine casualties, terrorism, natural and terrorist disaster relief, and marine firefighting, among other events. However, today, he'd decided to go up with this crew, observing their training mission out of Clearwater, home to the largest and busiest Air Station in the Coast Guard.

There were days he missed being on SAR missions—missed the adrenaline rush—so occasionally, he'd head out with one of the teams. A new rescue swimmer (RS) was recently transferred to their base after graduating from the USCG Aviation Survivalman "A" School and Emergency Medical Technician school. Stefan had been watching as Ensign Darren Jacoby had been put through his paces by Master Chief Josh Graves when the call for a real rescue had come in. Their chopper had been the closest to the area where the aircraft had gone down, so Stefan had ordered the pilots to head toward the coordinates. He then used his headset to contact the operations center to let them know he and the crew were responding.

The rescue was the first thing all day to get Stefan's mind completely off Cassie—something that had been impossible most days lately. He'd hoped to see her at the club last night, but she hadn't been there—probably swamped with schoolwork. He was still at a loss over the fact she'd declined to resign their contract three weeks ago. Everything had been going well, or at least he'd thought they'd been. He'd been more than willing to schedule playtime around her shifts at the hospital, classes, and schoolwork. She wasn't the first sub he'd had a D/s relationship with that'd lasted for more than a few weeks or months, but Stefan had been the one to end all the others.

*Hmm. Is that it? Am I upset things didn't end on my terms for once? Or is there something more to it?*

After his shift ended today, he needed to stop by The Covenant and talk to Mitch about which subs were available to help him with the Shibari class. He'd been putting it off, but the class started a week from Monday, and he wanted to practice with his new assistant at least once or twice before then. Unfortunately, he had little desire to use anyone other than Cassie, and that fact was driving him nuts. While he wouldn't be willing to start another contracted D/s relationship—not yet—he did need a sub in order to demonstrate to the Doms in the class the proper way to wrap their subs up in ropes. Whoever ended up being his assistant would be compensated for their time by the club's owners, as Cassie had been during the first class he'd taught earlier in the year. While Stefan had volunteered his time, Mitch Sawyer had insisted the sub be paid since the class was on Monday and Tuesday nights when the club was usually closed.

Cassie had always looked so good with Stefan's ropes enveloping her, sometimes from head to toe. He would've just barely started, but after the second or third knot, she'd already be in subspace. He'd never questioned her need for the ropes—that would've been too personal, something he avoided in his relationships over the last few years. Maybe it was for the best that Cass had ended things. He'd gotten too comfortable around her. During the last few months of their contracted relationship, one or two times per week, she'd stayed the night at his townhouse after they'd spent an evening playing. Stefan had awakened more than once on other mornings, reaching for her before realizing she wasn't there. A full-time relationship wasn't something he needed or wanted—maybe someday, but right now, his life was devoted to the Guard.

"Commander! Life raft in the water, two o'clock!" yelled the flight mechanic, Ensign Doyle Peters, who was perched next to Stefan, causing him to adjust the direction of his binoculars. Sure enough, there was a bright, yellow raft with two adults and two children wearing orange life vests and waving wildly at their soon-to-be rescuers. Thank God. There was no sign of the plane, but between the currents it could've been caught up in and the amount of time since it'd gone down, Stefan hadn't expected it to be near its former occupants. As long as they were safe, the plane no longer mattered.

The pilot, Lieutenant Vito LeBlanc, and his female co-pilot, Lieutenant Junior Grade Jodi Ziegler, acknowledged they also saw the raft, and the helo banked in that direction before dropping in altitude. Graves and Jacoby were already prepared to jump from the open side doors of the aircraft as soon as it was low enough. LeBlanc positioned the big bird in a hover over the waves, just far enough away from the raft so it wouldn't get caught in the rotors' downdraft. The water was choppy enough already, with the raft rocking back and forth, and they didn't want to add more to it.

Once Peters gave him the hand signal, Graves jumped out, feet first, arms crossed over his chest, a split second before Jacoby did the same. When they hit the water, they slipped under for a moment, then resurfaced and swam toward the raft, using strong strokes and the flippers on their feet. Stefan watched as the highly trained crew did what they did best. Ironically, the operation was similar to what he would've observed them doing during the practice run had it not been interrupted.

Once the rescue swimmers had reached the survivors, the helo gained some altitude, and LeBlanc repositioned it directly over the raft. Widening the distance from the water to the aircraft would result in a reduction in the strength of the downdraft, but it also increased the time the survivors would be in midair. It was one of those damned either-way actions.

As the hoist line was lowered, Jacoby removed his flippers and climbed into the raft with the family. With the father's help, he got the little girl, who looked about five years old, into a child-sized harness while her mother and slightly older brother waited their turns.

Graves kept a watchful eye on his new swimmer's actions. A storm was rolling in, dark clouds blocking out the sun. The wind had picked up, making the waves larger and more frequent, rocking the raft harder, and it took about two minutes for them to get the crying girl ready. It was clear she was terrified, and Stefan's heart broke for her.

Once she was secured in the harness, Jacoby attached her to his own harness before clipping them both onto the hoist line. Looking skyward, he gave Peters a thumbs up. Slowly, the winch lifted them into the air. They maintained a steady pace, and it wasn't too long before they were level with the helicopter's floor. Stefan helped the flight mechanic pull them onboard and unhook the girl from Jacoby so he could head back down for the next person.

Stefan wrapped the wet, shivering, and sobbing girl in a trauma blanket, then buckled her into one of the seats in the rear of the helo. He did his best to comfort her, which was hard to do over the noise of the thundering rotors. But he doubted she would settle down before the rest of her family was brought on board and they were back on dry land. Five minutes later, he repeated the process with the boy, who yelled that his name was Tommy Fischer and he was seven years old. He also told Stefan his sister's name was Emma.

Next up was their mother, Ruby. When Stefan tried to put a blanket around her, she threw her arms around him, thanking him profusely. Or at least he thought that's what she was saying. Between her sobs and the rotors, he couldn't really hear her. Once he had her secured next to her children, he turned his attention back to the last survivor being brought up. After Mark Fischer and Jacoby were safely onboard, the hoist line descended one last time for Graves.

While Jacoby got Mr. Fischer secured into a seat, Stefan moved back to the open door and watched the master chief make his assent. The storm was almost upon them, with lightning flashing through the sky. The wind worsened, causing Graves to spin faster and sway harder below the helo. They needed to get him onboard fast and head back toward the coast. None of them wanted to be caught in the middle of a thunderstorm if it could be avoided.

Graves was almost level with the door when there was a loud bang, and the winch suddenly jolted. The cable he was attached to snapped harshly and then began to unravel. The man's eyes ballooned as he realized he was about to fall about three or four stories. Stefan dove onto the floor, partially out the door, and grabbed onto Graves' arm just before he was out of reach. The master chief managed to clasp onto Stefan's arm simultaneously. Not a moment too soon, either, as the cable completely split in two. The only thing keeping Graves from falling and slamming onto the surface of the water like a ton of bricks was Stefan's grip.

A heavy weight crashed onto his legs and hips, and Stefan realized it was Jacoby. The rookie was preventing him from being dragged out of the helo. Peters was hooked onto a safety line and moved out onto the skid to try to grab Graves. Stefan's strained right arm and shoulder were screaming in pain, but there was no way he was letting go of the other man. The master chief's gaze met his, pure confidence in his expression that his LC wouldn't let him fall. Stefan hoped he wouldn't fail him.

Lightning flashed across the darkening skies, and the air crackled around them as Peters leaned down and, after several tries, managed to get ahold of the harness strap on Graves's shoulder. Working together, the two men hauled the master chief up and into the helo. He collapsed onto the floor next to Stefan, both breathing heavily. Stefan hesitantly moved his shoulder, ensuring it was still in its socket.

After a moment, Graves burst out laughing and slapped Stefan on his uninjured left shoulder. He yelled to be heard. "Thanks, LC! Good to know you're still quick on the draw! Drinks are on me tonight!"

Stefan chuckled as he rolled to his knees. He massaged his aching shoulder and arm. "I'm holding you to that, Master Chief! And it better be the good stuff!" Up front, both pilots were staring over their shoulders at the rest of the crew and the survivors. Stefan gave them a thumbs up. "Let's head home!"

Thirty minutes later, they were back on land. The Fischer family had been loaded into two ambulances and had probably already arrived at Largo Medical Center to be checked out. The mechanics at the air station had pulled the helicopter into a hanger, out of the rain, so they could try to figure out what'd happened to the winch. Several officers arrived and started the investigation process. Each member of the SAR crew and Stefan would have to give detailed reports. Hopefully, the incident wasn't due to human error. Every inch of the SAR helicopters and the equipment on board were routinely checked for wear and tear, but nothing was ever one hundred percent safe. Shit happened, and all they could do was pray no one was hurt or killed as a result.

While talking to his superior, Captain George Lowe, the Sector Commander, Stefan rubbed his left shoulder and arm. They ached, and he felt a tingling in his fingers. Oddly, his right arm and shoulder were the ones he'd strained to the limit, saving the master chief. Maybe he'd hurt his left side when he'd landed on the floor of the helo. Some Tylenol or Aleve should help.

"Stefan, you okay?" Lowe asked suddenly, eying him in concern. "You look pale."

"I'm fine, Captain." Actually, he didn't feel fine. In fact, a wave of dizziness came over him, and he swayed on his feet. A crushing pain flared under his ribs, to the left of his sternum, and Stefan clutched his chest. He heard shouts—however, they sounded far away. He tried to focus but found it impossible. A buzzing noise started and intensified in his ears as sweat beaded on his forehead. Stefan took one, maybe two, steps before his legs gave out. He hit his knees a moment before his world faded to black.

# Six

Cassandra pushed the portable electrocardiogram machine out of the elevator and down a long hallway. As part of her job description as a cardiac rehab tech, she was scheduled to cover one Saturday and an alternate Sunday shift per month, doing the daily EKGs doctors had ordered for their patients who'd been admitted. She was also on-call for any emergencies, which was why she was heading to the ER right now. Her beeper had gone off when she'd finished up in the surgical ICU, signaling they needed her on the first floor. Once she was done there, she'd return to cardiology and leave the stack of EKG printouts for review by the on-call doctor, who would be in around 1:00 p.m.

She would need to go through the hospital's computer system to see if any of the patients had gotten the test done at the hospital before for any reason. If so, she'd pull the file for the cardiologist so he could compare the past readings with the current one. If the patient had never had an EKG at Largo Medical Center before, then she'd make a new file for them.

The paperwork and data entry could be mundane, but she liked the other aspects of her job. Interacting with patients was what she enjoyed the most and was what influenced Cass to return to school to get her nursing degree. Between work and school, the next two years would be hectic, but she was looking forward to it. Thankfully, she'd already gotten her associate degree in liberal arts a few years ago, so the basic classes needed for her bachelor's were already taken care of.

Entering the ER, she found it bustling, busier than usual for 11:00 on a Saturday morning. It'd been quieter when Cass had been called down earlier for an elderly woman who'd been having trouble breathing. However, right before she'd left to finish her rounds upstairs, two ambulances had pulled up with a family of four who'd apparently been in a small plane that had crashed into the Gulf of Mexico. Thankfully, none of them had seemed badly injured—just some bumps and bruises. Now, Cass could see the parents sitting in chairs in the isolation room where their children lay on gurneys. The ER staff had probably put them in the rarely used room with two beds so they could be together.

Meanwhile, nurses, doctors, techs, and orderlies were either taking care of the numerous other patients they had or tackling the massive amount of paperwork and computer data entry that was required for each one. Currently, there was a lot of activity in the trauma room, but Cass wouldn't go in there unless they requested her. Checking the nurses' station, she found three EKG orders in their assigned slot in a file sorter. Two patients were in the general, non-critical section, while the third was in the Urgent Care room. The latter would be her first patient.

She had to wait for two EMTs with an empty gurney to pass before pushing her machine into Urgent Care. There were five beds in this area, and only two of them were occupied. In the last cubicle on the right, through an open curtain, she noticed the woman she'd tested earlier that morning was still there. Cass was glad to see she seemed to be breathing much easier and was either sleeping or relaxing with her eyes closed. Cass's current patient was two cubicles over.

Two men were standing outside the closed curtain, talking in low voices, so no one could overhear them. One was wearing the Coast Guard's Operational Dress Uniform—ODU—of navy-blue cargo pants and a matching button-down, short-sleeved shirt. The other man had on an orange jumpsuit that Cass knew the Search and Rescue team members wore. Both men stood over six feet tall and were quite handsome, but they didn't come close to how hot Master Stefan looked in his CG uniform. She'd seen him wearing his ODU on a few occasions and once in formal dress. The man was drool-worthy in whatever he wore but never more than in his uniforms. Okay, scratch that. His club leathers topped everything. His bad-boy Dom look made her heart beat faster than his clean-cut, military look. And, damn it, now she was daydreaming about Sir again—the man she loved who didn't love her back.

*Get a grip, Cass. You've got work to do.*

She steered her machine toward the two men, who stopped talking and eyed her. Pasting on a smile, Cass said, "Hi, I need to take an EKG if you don't mind waiting in the hallway. It'll only be a few minutes."

"Sure," the man in the ODU responded with a smile. "Take good care of the LC. He's a bit grumpy at the moment—he hates hospitals—but having a pretty woman like you working on him will have him feeling better in no time."

His kind expression and tone told her he'd meant the compliment in a good way and not salaciously. He wasn't hitting on her, but instead, just making conversation, probably out of worry for his coworker or friend.

Cass looked at him quizzically. "LC?"

"Lieutenant Commander."

"Ah." Actually, she'd known that. Master Stefan was a lieutenant commander in the Coast Guard, and in informal settings, people sometimes called him LC or just Commander. They couldn't call him lieutenant anymore since his promotion, even though it was part of his title, because that was a lower rank. A few people had made that mistake at the club and had been corrected by those who'd been in the military or still were.

"Okay, well, I'll do my best to have the LC in a better mood before I leave. Does he like knock-knock jokes?" She'd added that last part after realizing her comment could have alluded to something inappropriate would be happening behind the closed curtain.

Both men chuckled, and the one in the jumpsuit pulled the curtain back for her. "Give it a shot—you never know."

Lying on the gurney was a man with a sheet covering his legs and hips. A hospital gown lay on top of that as if he'd taken it off and thrown it there. An oxygen mask concealed his mouth and nose, while an IV catheter had been inserted into his right hand. A monitor above him beeped steadily as it displayed his oxygen saturation, respiration and heart rates, and blood pressure. Three EKG leads were attached to stickers on his chest—his very well-defined chest that was just as taut as his washboard abs. Damn, the man was fit.

Not surprisingly, he didn't move when Cass closed the curtains. His eyes were shut, and there was a good chance he was sleeping, so she moved quietly around the cubicle. After plugging the portable machine into an outlet in the wall behind him, Cass found the order for his EKG among the three she'd set aside. She glanced at the name so she could compare it to the one on the wristband he was wearing to make certain she had the correct patient.

"Oh, my God!" Her gaze flew to the man's face. It couldn't be . . . but now that she really looked at his face, it was him. Just to be sure, she eyed the tattoos on his left upper arm.

Her heart clenched when she realized they were the ones she'd seen every time he'd gone shirtless at the club or his place. The top one was an eagle, American flag, and anchor montage with USCG in block lettering. Below that, over his thick bicep, was another tattoo of a knotted rope that encircled his arm.

Her gaze returned to his face as she gently touched his right forearm. "Master Stefan?"

His eyelids lifted, and he blinked a few times. He *had* been asleep, and she'd woken him. "Cassie?"

His voice was muffled by the mask. Reaching up, he pulled it away from his mouth and nose and tucked it below his chin. Despite the extra oxygen, there was an ashen appearance to his skin she hadn't noticed right away.

"What're you doing here?" His voice was raspy, and he cleared his throat.

"I was just going to ask you that, Sir. W-what happened?" Even though they weren't in a D/s situation, Cass had immediately reverted to using the proper title with him since she'd rarely seen or spoken to him outside of the club or his townhouse when they were playing. Old habits die hard.

Sir shifted on the thin mattress. "Can you lift the back of this thing for me?"

"I can, after I do an EKG, but tell me why you're here. What's wrong?" Without waiting for him to answer, she scanned the paper she still held. Under his name, date of birth, and some other information was the section that said why the test had been ordered.

Possible MI.

*Oh shit.* MI stood for myocardial infarction, otherwise known as a heart attack! Master Stefan was too young and healthy for that, wasn't he? But Cass knew from experience that cardiac disease didn't discriminate. Her father had died from an MI at the age of thirty-nine. Her uncle had passed away from the same thing three years later, at the same age his older brother had been.

A shiver shot through her. The thought of the handsome, vibrant man in front of her dying scared the hell out of her.

---

When he'd opened his eyes, Stefan had experienced a fleeting thought he was dead and a stunning angel was welcoming him into the afterlife. Even in hospital scrubs, with her hair up in a ponytail and wearing minimal makeup, Cassandra Myers was still one of the sexiest women he'd ever known.

After moving to Tampa and passing the background checks to join The Covenant, he'd spent over a year or so playing with different submissives, getting to know them and seeing how they responded to his ropes. Cassie had been his favorite, even though it'd been understood there would be no strings attached—no pun intended.

They'd always played at the club or his townhouse. In fact, he'd never gone to her apartment or out on a date with her. No dinner in restaurants or movies or non-sexual things other couples did. The closest they'd ever come to an actual date was dinner at his place, then some playtime with a few orgasms, followed by aftercare while watching TV. And now, for the first time since they'd signed their initial contract, he regretted keeping her at arm's length. He missed his little pixie.

Fear flashed across her face when she read something on the paper she was holding, and he tried to reassure her he was perfectly fine. Rolling his eyes, he sighed. "It's nothing serious, Cassie, just indigestion or something. No big deal. I'm sure I'll be discharged as soon as the doctor gets a chance to fill out the paperwork."

The expression on her face told him she didn't believe him

any more than the emergency room doctor had during his examination when he'd basically told him the same thing. It hadn't helped that Stefan's blood pressure had been 210/130 at the time—far higher than his average 110/70. The physician had ordered a nurse to give Stefan a tiny nitroglycerin pill, and it hadn't been long before the pain shooting through his chest and down his arm had dissipated. His blood pressure had dropped to more reasonable numbers as well.

Stefan wasn't stupid. If his symptoms hadn't been cardiac-related, the nitro wouldn't have done a damn thing to relieve them. He just didn't want to face what that meant. If he was having heart trouble, his career was at stake.

"Sir—"

"It's Stefan while we're here, Cassie, and I'm fine. Do what you have to do."

Her lips pursed, and after a moment's hesitation, she turned toward her machine and proceeded to set up for the test. As she put stickers with silver knobs on them onto specific spots on his chest, he studied her and tried to ignore how good it felt to have her touch him, even though she was being professionally clinical about it. Not knowing the difference, his cock twitched, and he willed the bastard not to respond.

"How's nursing school going?" Yeah, he was making routine small talk, but he really did miss her. While he'd paid for her membership at The Covenant, he hadn't seen her there since her last shift as a waitress a little over a week ago. Mitch, Devon, and Ian had gotten a good-luck cake to celebrate her last night and new adventure. They'd also given her an eyebrow-raising monetary gift to put towards her tuition.

She glanced at him in surprise. "Um . . . it's going well. I like it."

"What courses are you taking this semester?"

"Since I'm going at night, I only have three classes—Intro

to Biology, Intro to Nursing, and Biochemistry. A lot of my basic courses are out of the way from my associate degree, but there are a few I need to take before I can start clinicals because they would've been part of my first year if I was starting from scratch. I'll be able to start clinicals next semester."

"Great. That's—that's good to hear. I have to admit, I miss—"

His pretty pixie spun back toward the machine on wheels. "Sorry, Sir—Stefan—but I need you to be quiet for a moment—breath normally and don't move."

"Uh . . . sure."

If he hadn't been mistaken, there had been a flash of pain in her eyes before she'd pivoted away from him. He wondered what was bothering her, but when she glanced back at him, her expression was blank. Maybe he'd been mistaken. After letting out a sigh, he did as she'd requested.

Cassie pushed a few buttons, and the machine began to spit out a paper copy of his EKG. After it stopped, she tore the paper at the perforations and stared at it for a moment. He asked, "How's it look?"

She gave him a weak smile. "Sorry, but the cardiologist gets to decide that. I just run the tests."

For some reason, he didn't think that was the whole truth. Otherwise, she wouldn't have been studying it so intently. But he doubted he could say anything to get her to admit that. She probably couldn't tell him anyway. He'd had plenty of X-rays, and the techs always told him they couldn't read them—the orthopedist had to. Most likely, it was hospital protocol. They couldn't have a technician saying one thing only to have the doctor's diagnosis be something completely different.

After unhooking the wires, she removed the stickers from his chest. "Um—Sir—I mean, Stefan, can I call someone for you? Family? Friends? I know there are two men from the Coast Guard here, but I—"

Stefan groaned. She had to be referring to Captain Lowe and Master Chief Graves, who'd followed his ambulance to the hospital. He'd regained consciousness to find Graves, Jacoby, and two paramedics working on him. He hadn't stopped breathing—he'd only fainted. Once they put an oxygen mask on him, he'd come around. The pain in his chest had still been there, but far less intense than it had been moments earlier—it'd become more of an ache than anything else at that point. It wasn't until after he'd arrived at the ER that it'd flared again, prompting the ER physician to order nitroglycerin.

"They're still here? I told them I was fine, and they could head back to the station." Of course, it'd been a suggestion, not an order, since Lowe was Stefan's superior.

When he shifted again, trying to get comfortable, Cass squeezed a handle underneath the top of the bed, and the upper half of his body rose until it was at a forty-five-degree angle or so.

"Is that better?" she asked. "Or do you want to go higher?"

"A little higher, if you don't mind."

She did it again, and he told her to stop when the position was to his liking. "That's good. Thanks. As for calling someone—no, you don't need to—shoot. Damn it, I forgot. I'm supposed to do a demo tonight at the club, and I left my phone in my truck at the air station. Can you call Mitch Sawyer and let him know I have to reschedule? I probably won't be up for it, even after they release me. Tell him I'm fine and there's nothing to worry about. I'll call him tomorrow."

"Um—sure. I can do that. Is there—is there anything else I can do for you?"

He shook his head, even though he wanted to ask her to sit and stay with him for a while. Not because he was scared or anything, but because he didn't want her to leave just yet. But she was working and didn't have time to hold his hand and fuss over him. "Nope, that's all I need for now. Thank you."

Cassie pulled the plug from the wall, wrapped the cord up, and hung it on a hook on the side of the machine. "I'll—uh—I'll check back with you in a bit. I'm working until three."

"Really, Cassie, you don't have to. I'm sure you've got plenty of work to do, and like I said, I'm sure the doc will be booting me out of here in a bit. No worries. Don't come back just to see me."

Her face fell, and Stefan felt like he'd kicked her dog if she had one. Before he could say anything else, though, the curtain opened, and one of the nurses entered the cubicle. "How're you feeling, Mr. Lundquist? Any pain?"

Stefan tried to smile, but as he watched Cassie leave with her machine, the corners of his mouth refused to move. "No —no pain."

Except for the one in his gut, now that his little pixie was gone.

# Seven

Cass left the ICU cubicle after performing a second EKG on an elderly woman who'd been admitted for a stroke and had then developed an arrhythmia about thirty minutes ago. When Cass had returned to the cardiology department earlier to process the morning's EKGs, her beeper had gone off again for the new order. She hadn't needed to bring a machine with her since the critical care units and the ER had their own.

She stopped at the nurses' station to see if there were any more orders. Finding none, she returned the EKG machine to its usual spot by a nearby wall, then stepped into the supply room to replenish the dwindling stock of leads—the stickers the EKG wires were connected to.

Unable to get her mind off Stefan, Cass had been on autopilot for the past hour. Once she'd finished the other two orders in the ER, she'd fought the urge to check in on him and had returned to the cardiology department. Before processing all the EKGs she'd performed since that morning, Cass had done as requested and contacted Mitch Sawyer. What she hadn't done was tell him that it was "just indigestion," as Stefan had tried to insist.

She'd been able to read his EKG more than she admitted to him. There'd been abnormalities in the thin lines on the graph which coincided with the electrical output of his heart. While the cardiologist would have to confirm it, Cass was pretty sure Stefan had suffered an MI and wouldn't be going home from the ER as he hoped.

She hadn't told Mitch about the probable heart attack. Instead, she'd related how Stefan had been brought in with chest pain but didn't want to worry anyone. He'd only wanted to cancel his demonstration tonight. Yeah, Sir was probably going to be pissed at her when Mitch showed up to check on him like he'd told her he would, but she'd deal with that later. Cass knew from past conversations that Stefan didn't have any close family living in the area—they lived in the Northeast—so it was up to his friends to be his support system in Florida. And if she was correct about the MI, then he was definitely going to need all the support he could get.

"Hey, beautiful. I didn't know you were working today." The deep, rumbling voice came from over Cass's shoulder as she placed the packages of leads into their correct slot on the side of the EKG machine. The words had been spoken close to her ear and had startled her for a moment before she relaxed again. Turning around, she smiled at the big man.

Randall West, one of the hospital's respiratory therapists, was extremely good-looking and reminded her of the actor Shemar Moore. Unfortunately, he was a bit of a player and a huge flirt, although not in a creepy way. Cass didn't think there was a single female coworker, patient, or visitor who didn't blush and smile whenever Randall turned on the charm, which he often did. However, even if his flirting and dating throughout the hospital hadn't been a problem for her, he also didn't give off a Dom vibe. The one she'd come to easily recognize in men over the years since joining the BDSM community. The one she needed in any relationships or brief encounters now. The one she craved. Despite all that, Randall always did brighten her day whenever she ran into him at the hospital.

"Yup, I am. I'm surprised I haven't seen you before now. I've been in every unit more than once today, except for maternity and pediatrics."

"The place is definitely hopping." He sat at the nurses' station and began typing on a computer keyboard, probably entering a treatment he'd performed on a patient. As he worked, he glanced her way and gave her his signature smile and a teasing wink. Cass knew exactly what was coming next. "So, when are you going to put me out of my misery and agree to go on a date with me, huh?"

"Hmm. Let's see. How about two years from now? That's when I'll be done with the nursing program, and I'll have more than five minutes to do something other than work, go to class, and do a ton of homework."

He chuckled. "I'll pencil you in." Pantomiming, he made a note in an invisible date book. "Two years from today, and I'm holding you to it. So, how's school going?"

Cass had told several people at the hospital that she'd gone back to get her nursing degree. Once she enrolled in school again, she'd been so excited about starting her classes that she kind of blurted it out during random conversations. Everyone had been happy for her and very encouraging.

"It's going good. It took a little bit to get back into a studying routine, but I'm really enjoying it."

"Glad to hear it. You're going to make a helluva nurse. You're great with people, and one only has to watch you for a minute to know you love working with patients."

His compliment had her heart swelling in her chest. She really did love taking care of patients and interacting with them—this wasn't *just* a job to her—and it was nice to hear someone else had noticed how much it meant to her. "Thanks, Randall."

The overhead speakers of the PA system came to life. "Code Ninety-Nine, Emergency Room. Code Ninety-Nine, Emergency Room."

At the alert of a cardiac arrest, Randall jumped to his feet. As the on-call respiratory tech, he was required to respond to all emergencies where the patient had stopped breathing or was having difficulty getting adequate air into their lungs and needed to be intubated and placed on a ventilator.

Rounding the corner of the nurses' desk, he gave Cass's shoulder two pats as he strode quickly past her. "Catch you later, beautiful."

Cass waved in his direction, but then she froze as the last few seconds came back to her in a rush.

*Code Ninety-Nine. Emergency Room. Cardiac Arrest. Master Stefan. Heart Attack. Oh, no, no, no, no, no! It can't be him!*

Her own heart pounded in her chest. While it could be any one of the numerous patients in the ER, Cass had a dark feeling of dread.

After making sure she'd left a copy of the EKG she'd done for the nurses to put in the patient's file, Cass hurried toward the door to the stairs Randall had taken a moment ago. She ran down the three flights to the ER faster than if she'd taken the elevator. Exiting into the hallway, her heart sank, and she became nauseous when she saw all the activity near the Urgent Care room. While members of the medical team rushed in and out of the room, Cass spotted the two men in uniform from earlier. With them were Masters Mitch and Ian. The grave expressions on their faces said her instincts had been correct. Stefan had gone into cardiac arrest.

Her feet felt like they were encased in cement blocks as she trod slowly toward the small group. As if sensing her presence, Ian turned, and his worried gaze met hers. When he closed the distance between them and opened his arms for her, she collapsed into his embrace, tears bursting forth. Ian held her tightly and murmured words of comfort that she couldn't comprehend. All she could think about was they were performing CPR on the man she loved. Oh, God, how she loved him. He couldn't die—he just couldn't. It would destroy her.

Trying to regain her composure, she lifted her head from Ian's shoulders, and he pulled back a few inches to look down at her. His startling blue eyes assessed her in an instant. "Are you okay, little one?"

Cass shook her head because she didn't trust her voice wouldn't send her into another crying bout just yet. Mitch stepped over and ran a strong hand up and down her back, but he didn't say anything. There were no attempts at false hope from either man, only solace, and for that, she was grateful.

She wasn't sure how long they'd stood there before she saw one of the hospital's cardiologists, Dr. Jonathan Chang, exit the Urgent Care room and tuck a stethoscope into the pocket of his white lab coat. A nurse was by his side as he gave out orders. "Let's get another twelve-lead EKG on him and cardiac enzymes. Put a catheter in, then call the OR and get an anesthesiologist down here. Tell them we'll do an angiogram as soon as he's stable. Are there any family members here?" He glanced around.

The two men from the Coast Guard stepped toward him. Ian, Mitch, and Cass hurried over as one of the men introduced himself to the doctor with a handshake. "I'm Captain

Lowe, and this is Master Chief Graves. We're with the lieutenant commander."

The doctor shook both men's hands. "Captain. Master Chief. I'm Dr. Chang from cardiology."

The captain handed him a manila file folder. "This is Stefan's full medical history from the base—it was just delivered. He doesn't have any family locally, but I'll make sure they're notified as soon as possible. Earlier, he gave the ER physician permission to keep us informed about his condition. How is he?"

Chang took a deep breath and let it out in a frustrated huff. "Well, he had a massive MI and went into cardiac arrest, but we got his heart started again after a few shocks with the defibrillator. He's been intubated and put on a ventilator to assist his breathing, and once he's stabilized, he'll be taken to the OR. An angiogram will tell us what our next steps will be —either angioplasty, a stent, or a bypass. We're doing everything we can, but I have to ask if he has advanced directives concerning his treatment."

Cass felt the blood drain from her face. She couldn't think about things becoming so dire they would stop all life-saving efforts if Stefan had indicated they should in case he appeared to be completely and permanently incapacitated. Cass was grateful when, simultaneously, Ian put his arm around her shoulders and Mitch grabbed her by the waist. It was as if they'd sensed her knees had been about to buckle.

"All that's in his file," Lowe responded somberly. "Is it that bad?"

The cardiologist shook his head. "No, I don't think it is— I'm just being cautious. Aside from whatever blockage is going on in his arteries, he's in good physical condition, which will definitely be an advantage. Of course, I'll know more after we get him to the OR. I'll keep you updated."

"Thanks, Doctor." The men shook hands again before

Chang walked away. Lowe and Graves exchanged looks of concern with each other and then the Sawyer cousins. Obviously, they either had all known each other before today, or Ian and Mitch had been there long enough for the four men to get somewhat acquainted. None of them said anything and the tense silence hung heavily in the air.

"Oh, Cass, there you are. I was just about to page you." She looked up to see one of the ER nurses approaching with a piece of paper in her hand. "We need a STAT cardiogram on bed three in UC."

Seemingly unaware of Cass's stress and familiarity with the man in Urgent Care, the nurse handed her the order and then hurried away.

Ian squeezed Cass's shoulder. "Are you going to be okay, Cassandra?"

She hesitated before nodding. Despite the fact she was scared spitless Stefan might die, she had a job to carry out. She was part of the team that would do everything they could to keep the man alive, even if she only had a small role in it. Pushing aside her personal feelings for professional ones, she cleared her throat. "Um . . . yes, Sir—Ian. I'm good."

His frown said he didn't believe her, but when she straightened her spine, both he and Mitch released her.

After retrieving one of the two EKG machines from where they sat when not in use, she wheeled it into the Urgent Care room. The curtains to Stefan's cubicle were wide open as the nurses and techs continued to work on him. Either Randall or one of the doctors had intubated him, and the respiratory therapist was now adjusting the settings on the machine that was forcing air into Stefan's lungs.

Cass stood frozen in place momentarily as she stared at the limp, unresponsive man. Her heart was in her throat while she watched his chiseled chest rise and fall through artificial means. Dr. Chang was one of the best cardiologists in the state of Florida, and if Cass had been the one lying on a gurney, suffering a heart attack, he was the one she'd want working on her. Stefan was in good hands, but he could also use whatever divine intervention Cass could conjure up. It'd been a while since she'd attended church, but once Stefan was in surgery, she'd visit the hospital's chapel, light a candle, and pray as she'd never prayed before.

# Eight

Little Peyton Sawyer slept soundly on her father's shoulder as Ian and several family members and friends sat in the surgical waiting room, along with a bunch of Coasties, eagerly anticipating news on Stefan. Ian had convinced his wife, Angie, he could handle his three-month-old daughter on his own for a while, so she could gather with the other women comforting Cassandra on the other side of the room. The young submissive had obviously developed strong feelings for the man who'd been her Dom for nine or ten months, and she was having a rough time right now.

After she finished her shift, she'd come directly here, still dressed in her hospital scrubs. Somehow, she'd managed to hold it together until she'd spotted Angie, Ian's sister-in-law Kristen, Shelby Christensen, and Sasha Lewis, and then she'd burst out crying. Her fellow submissives and friends had immediately gone into support warrior mode, taking care of her. It was something they all did well.

Ian had been a bit surprised when Stefan had informed him Cassandra declined to renew their monthly contract a few weeks ago. He'd known the Dom for almost two years now, and they'd also become friends outside the club. Ian, a retired Navy SEAL, liked to give the other man shit for being a Coastie and got it right back in return. Rivalries between the different branches of the military were standard, but when it really mattered, they always had each other's backs.

While getting to know the lieutenant commander after he'd joined The Covenant, Ian discovered how talented the man was with Shibari. He created amazing and intricate designs on submissives and had become a club favorite for demonstrations, his rope scenes always drawing a crowd. From the beginning, Ian had thought Master Stefan would be the perfect Dom for Cassandra. However, the man had spent some time playing with several subs who liked to be tied up in ropes, not committing to any of them. When he'd finally signed a contract with Cassandra, even though it was for one month at a time, it looked like an ideal match had been made. But for some reason, a few weeks ago, it'd all come to an end, and Ian believed both of them had made a huge mistake in terminating their D/s relationship.

Ian had only played with Cassandra that one night at the club, about four-and-a-half years ago before he'd met his beautiful wife. He'd been happy to help her on her path of discovery in the world of BDSM, but he'd wanted her to find a Dom who could give her more than just satisfying her basic need to be restrained. Ian had thought Stefan would be that Dom, and he still believed it—they were good together, even if they didn't realize it yet.

After the man pulled through surgery—and he would, damn it—he'd have to make major changes to his life, whether he wanted to or not. Maybe whatever had been holding him and Cassandra back from each other would shift in another direction. One could only hope.

It was a little after 10:00 p.m. when an older couple walked into the Cardiac Care Unit's waiting room, escorted by Master Chief Graves, and looked around. Stefan's parents had gotten the first available flight from Connecticut to be by their son's side after Captain Lowe had contacted them. Cassandra recognized them immediately from a few pictures Stefan had scattered about his apartment, but she just realized she'd never learned their first names.

Mr. Lundquist was a handsome man—tall and physically fit, with salt-and-pepper hair and soft, brown eyes—and it was easy to see where Stefan had gotten his good looks. His mother was an elegant woman with green eyes and blonde hair who complemented her husband well. The two of them made a stunning couple.

Cass wondered why Stefan's sister hadn't come too. From the little she knew of his family, his older sister—Elin, if Cass remembered correctly—also lived in Connecticut, near their parents. She thought Stefan and Elin were relatively close, despite the physical distance between them, so there had to be a reason the woman wasn't there, worrying about her brother like everyone else.

The only people still in the waiting room for Stefan were Cassandra, Sasha, and Ian. The rest of his friends and coworkers had gone home after receiving word he'd pulled through the surgery and was in stable condition. A stent had been put in place to increase the blood flow through the artery that had apparently been ninety-five percent blocked, which had caused the MI. Dr. Chang had told Captain Lowe he'd ordered an MRI for tomorrow to try to assess the damage the heart attack had caused. He was optimistic Stefan would make a full recovery over time with rehab.

Although she'd been incredibly relieved to hear Stefan

would be okay, Cass was now worried for a different reason. While Stefan was still in surgery, she'd overheard Captain Lowe and Master Chief Graves talking in the hallway. Apparently, there was a good chance Stefan would have to take a medical discharge from the Coast Guard. She knew he'd be crushed if that happened. He was so proud to be a USCG officer and loved what he did. At the age of thirty-eight, what would he do if he couldn't be a Coastie? He didn't even have his twenty years of service in yet. From what she knew, he had four more years to go and had planned to stay in the USCG for many years after that. He was too young to be retired.

Master Chief Graves brought Mr. and Mrs. Lundquist over to the trio and gestured toward them. "John and Stina Lundquist, these are some of Stefan's good friends. This is Ian Sawyer, Cassandra Myers, and Sasha Lewis." The master chief and captain had gotten to know some of the club members who'd arrived while Stefan had still been in surgery. But as far as Cass could tell, neither man was in the lifestyle, nor were the two aware of how they'd all known Stefan and from where. None of the Doms or subs would've let that cat out of the bag, especially to his superior. If Stefan wanted anyone from the Coast Guard or his family to know he was a practicing Dom, then he'd be the one to tell them.

After everyone had shaken hands, Ian said, "Stefan's been stable since he's gotten out of surgery. We didn't want to leave until after you'd arrived to make sure you didn't need anything. I know the cardiologist is in CCU right now—I think he had another patient admitted. I'll go tell him you're here, and he can give you a full update."

"Thank you," John replied. "I understand there were a lot more of you earlier. Stina and I appreciate everyone being here for our son in lieu of his family. It made us feel more at ease knowing he was supported by good friends and coworkers until we could get here. I know he loves living in Florida, but it doesn't make things easy when something like this happens."

Ian nodded. "I hear you. In fact, my own folks are in the process of moving here from North Carolina since my brothers and I all live in Tampa. They have two grandkids now and couldn't stand being that far away." He jutted his chin toward the door. "Let me get the doctor for you."

"I'll do it, Ian," Cass found herself saying. It had taken her a few hours to be more comfortable not saying Master in front of his name and those of a few other Doms who'd been there earlier. She wasn't used to seeing them outside of the club or at a lifestyle party. Looking at Ian, she held up her ID badge, which was also an electronic key. "At this time of night, you'd have to get buzzed in, and they're probably busy getting ready for shift change. I'll let Dr. Chang know Mr. and Mrs. Lundquist are here."

Stefan's mother smiled at her. "Thank you . . . Cassandra, was it?"

"Yes, ma'am. Although a lot of people have shortened it to Cass, and Stefan calls me Cassie. I'll respond to any and all versions of my name." She didn't know why she'd said all that when a simple "yes" could have sufficed, but when she was nervous or scared, she tended to babble a bit.

The woman's smile broadened, and there was a twinkle in her eye, despite her worry for Stefan, when she declared, "I like Cassie—it's pretty and suits you. And please, call us Stina and John. There's no need for formalities among friends."

Cass adored her immediately. She was the type of mother who'd probably ensured her children's friends always knew they were welcome at her house when they'd been younger and in school. And most likely still did so. "If you insist, then Stina and John it is. And Stefan said the same thing when we first met, and he decided to call me Cassie."

She stepped toward the door leading to the hallway. "I'll

let Dr. Chang know you're here. He's very nice and one of the top cardiologists in the state."

When she saw a flash of relief on Stefan's parents' faces, she was glad she'd given their son's physician a glowing endorsement. Knowing Stefan was being well taken care of by one of the best would hopefully ease their worry a little bit.

Soon after, Dr. Chang updated Stefan's parents on his condition and then let them see him for a few minutes, even though he was sleeping. Once the couple returned to the waiting room, Sasha and Ian took their leave after making sure the Lundquists didn't need anything. The commander had arranged for them to have a room at a hotel nearby. The Coast Guard would surely take good care of Stina and John during this difficult time. But just in case, Ian had given them his card with his personal cell number on it, telling them they could call him as well for anything at all. He also informed them that he and several of Stefan's non-CG friends would be in and out of the hospital over the next few days, checking on both him and them. The couple was extremely grateful for all the support they were receiving.

When Stina and John mentioned they'd be staying in the waiting room for a little bit since the nurses had promised to let them know if Stefan woke up, Cass decided to keep them company. Truthfully, she was afraid if she went home, something terrible would happen again. Stefan had already suffered a massive heart attack and had gone into cardiac arrest in the ER. What if that happened again in the CCU? She knew she wasn't being completely rational—Dr. Chang had assured them the blockage had been cleared and Stefan should be moved to the step-down cardiac unit as early as Monday. But Cass was still worried she'd go home and then return to find out he was gone—as in never-coming-back gone.

"Can I get you some coffee or tea, Stina? John? There's both, in regular and decaf, if you don't want the caffeine keeping you awake later." She indicated the little station set up on the other side of the room. There was a Keurig hooked up to a constant water source, assorted coffee and tea pods, packets of sugar and substitutes, some honey, and a small refrigerator that held milk and creamers.

"Oh, I would love a cup of decaf tea," Stina announced as she got comfortable on one of the room's loveseats. "With a little bit of honey, if that's what I see next to the machine. Thank you, Cassie."

"You're more than welcome. John?"

"No, thank you, Cassie. I'm fine." Stefan's father smiled wearily at her before bending at the waist and giving his wife a gentle kiss on her temple. "You two chat. I'm going to walk the hallway for a bit and stretch my legs. They're still stiff from the flight."

A few minutes later, Cass handed Stina a hot cup of tea with a dollop of honey. "Thank you, dear." After the woman took it from her, she patted the cushion next to her. "Please, have a seat if you insist on staying for a little while—which you really don't have to do."

"It's no trouble. Besides, this is like a second home to me. Once in a while, when I'm lying in bed at night, my apartment seems too quiet. You'd think it would be welcoming after working in a busy hospital all day, but it really isn't sometimes."

"Which department do you work in?"

"Ironically, cardiology. Actually, I'm a cardiac rehab tech. I just have to work one Saturday and one Sunday a month doing EKGs, which is what I was doing today when I got called to the ER to find my patient was Stefan."

Stina took a sip of tea and swallowed. "Mmm, that's good. That must have been quite a shock for you." When Cass nodded in agreement, the woman continued. "May I ask you something?"

"Of course." Cass figured it would be a medical question, but it turned out she was wrong.

"Are you and Stefan dating?"

Her mouth dropped as her eyes rounded. "Um . . . no—no, we're not. We're just . . . um . . . friends. Good friends."

Well, they were . . . sort of. She couldn't very well tell his mother Stefan had been her Dom for ten months, tying her up in Shibari ropes before fucking her until she screamed his name as the most intense orgasms of her life tore through her. Nope, she definitely couldn't say all that.

"But you wish you were more than just friends, don't you? You don't need to answer that—I can see it on your face. While everyone else is worried, you're terrified about what's happened to him, but you're trying to hide it." Reaching over, Stina took Cass's hand and squeezed it. "He's going to be fine, Cassie. You'll see."

She *had* been trying to hide her emotions and was shocked Stina had seen through her facade as easily as Ian and the other Doms had. They all knew her well and knew how to read a person's body language better than most people. She hadn't even attempted to lie to any of them earlier, trying to pass herself off as just another concerned friend of Stefan's. In those moments, they'd known the truth. That submissive Cassandra was in love with Master Stefan.

# NINE

A constant beeping dragged a reluctant Stefan from his sleep, and he blinked several times before the room came into focus. Blue curtains. Scratchy, white sheets and blanket. IV pole. Antiseptic stench. Oxygen flowing from a cannula in his nose. Small TV on an adjustable arm. Feeling like he'd been run over by a Mack truck. Okay, he was alive. That was good, right?

The last thing he remembered was being in the ER, and what? He'd been there for chest pain, and the doctor had given him a pill that made it go away, right? His mind raced, trying to recall the details. Nitroglycerin—that was it. What'd happened after that?

An image of Cassie, dressed in scrubs, floated into his brain—his beautiful pixie. No, not his. She'd given him his collar back, so she was no longer his.

*You idiot. She never was. You made sure she knew your whole time together was temporary and always had an end date. Never thought she'd be the one to break it off, did you? Dumbass.*

The blood pressure cuff wrapped around his upper arm began to inflate as he inspected the area he was in. It wasn't an actual room but a cubicle. However, it didn't look like the one in the ER, and while there were definitely people moving around on the other side of the curtain, it wasn't as busy. When had he been transferred? And where was he now?

The blue curtain opened with a *swish*, and a scrub-clad woman strode in. The tall brunette smiled when she saw him. "You're awake—good. I'm Nancy, your nurse for the next several hours. How are you feeling?"

"Ok—" Stefan coughed on the word because his mouth and throat were parched, and pain flared in his chest. It didn't feel like the last time, though, but he couldn't remember when that was.

Nancy poured water from a plastic pitcher into a cup, then added a straw. Before giving it to him, she pushed a button on the side rail of the bed, and his upper torso began to rise at an angle. "Is that comfortable?" When he nodded, she brought the straw to his lips. "Drink up, but not too quickly."

The cool liquid felt like heaven as he swallowed it down. After drinking his fill, he relaxed back onto the pillow.

"What happened?" he asked, happy his voice was almost back to normal.

"Well, according to the report I received this morning, you had an angiogram yesterday that resulted in them putting a stent in."

"Stent? Why?" His uncle had gotten a stent put in his heart last year after developing unstable angina. But the man was seventy-six years old. Stefan was half his age. Maybe they put stents in other parts of the body, too, and not just in the heart. He was healthy as a horse. Or at least he thought he was.

"Dr. Chang, your cardiologist, will be here shortly to explain everything to you." She stuck a probe in his ear and took his temperature. "For now, just relax."

He snorted as she wrote several numbers down on a chart after noting his vitals on the monitor. "Easier said than done.

You're not the one hooked up to a bunch of monitors and an IV, with oxygen tubing stuck up your nose."

"And a urine catheter. Don't forget about that sucker."

Stefan gaped at her in horror, then slowly lifted the blanket and sheets covering his body just enough to see his crotch. He gingerly pulled the bottom of the hospital gown someone had put on him up and out of the way.

*Well, hell. That sucks.* Good thing he didn't remember it going in. He shivered at the thought and prayed it wouldn't hurt like a bitch when it came out.

"Gee, thanks."

Nancy patted his shoulder. "You'll be fine. Are you hungry? The breakfast trays just arrived."

"Is it edible?"

"The tray? No. The breakfast?" She grinned and shrugged. "Honestly, it's not half bad for hospital food. I'll bring one in, and you can give it a try. We also have yogurts and other quick and easy foods in the pantry."

"Nurse Nancy, you've got a helluva sense of humor," he said dryly. "We'll get along just fine as long as you're gentle when that damn catheter comes out."

"Oh, I won't be doing that. That's Big Jim's job."

His jaw went slack as she walked out of the cubicle, then he shook his head. Hopefully, she'd been kidding about "Big Jim." There was no way he wanted some guy named Big Jim—or any guy for that matter—pulling a tube out of his junk, much less touching it.

After his breakfast arrived, Stefan picked at the lump of dry eggs before passing on them. The pile of fresh fruit was pretty good, and the bowl of oatmeal was tolerable. If he hadn't been so hungry, he would've waited to see if lunch was any better.

Once he was finished eating, he pushed the rolling bedside tray to the side. Glancing around the bed, he found the remote that controlled the TV. Turning it on, he watched the local news for a few minutes before a man wearing glasses and a lab coat strode in and held out his hand. "Stefan, I'm Dr. Chang. I doubt you remember me from yesterday—you were in bad shape there for a bit."

Stefan shook his hand. "How bad? I barely remember anything. I know I had chest pain after a rescue, but it went away when they gave me nitroglycerin in the ER."

The man leaned against the bedrail and crossed his arms. "And about an hour later, you had a massive MI—a heart attack—and went into full cardiac arrest. We had to shock you three times before we got your heart started again. You're very lucky you were already in the ER when that happened."

Stunned, he gawked at the man. "Holy sh . . . are you saying I was . . . I almost *died* yesterday?"

Chang nodded. "As I said, you were very lucky. We had to intubate you and put you on a ventilator. Once you were stabilized, we took you to the OR for an angiogram. One of the main arteries of your heart was ninety-five percent blocked with plaque. We cleared most of it out and put a stent in that part of the artery to restore the blood flow. I had them remove the intubation tube before transferring you here from recovery since your vitals were good, and you could breathe on your own. This morning, I'm sending you for an MRI to assess the extent of the damage from the MI. You'll be hospitalized for a few days, but your prognosis is good. Before you're released, we'll do a stress test and see how you handle it." He bent his elbows, lifting his hands and flashing his palms. "I think that about covers it. Any questions?"

Yeah, he had a lot of them, but the biggest was the one he couldn't voice. What did this mean for his career? A massive heart attack could result in a medical discharge from the Coast Guard, and it wouldn't be his decision.

*Damn it. This can't be happening.*

He shook his head as his gaze dropped to his lap. "No, not yet. I'm sure I'll have a few after this all sinks in."

"No problem. While you're waiting for them to come get you for the MRI, I've ordered some blood work and an EKG." He pulled a stethoscope from his coat pocket and unraveled it before putting the earpieces in. "Just going to take a listen." He placed the instrument's bell under Stefan's thin hospital gown, over his heart. "Breathe normally." After a few seconds, he moved it a few inches. "Deep breath." After Stefan complied, the bell was moved again. "Another . . . good."

Standing erect again, Chang removed the stethoscope from his ears. "Okay. We'll get those tests done, and I'll be back to check on you later. For now, you're on bed rest. Maybe this afternoon, you'll be allowed to sit in the chair for a bit." He pointed to an ugly, yellow recliner on the other side of the cubicle before adding, "Once I get the test results back, I'll see about sending you to the step-down unit, all right?"

"Yeah, that's fine, Doc. Thanks," Stefan replied absentmindedly. His mind was still reeling from everything he'd been told. Holy shit, he'd had a fucking heart attack and almost died! At thirty-eight years old!

*Damn it!*

---

Taking a deep breath, Cass steeled herself to maintain her composure before sliding the curtain out of the way and entering the cubicle. Stefan's eyes had been shut, but they opened at the faint noise. His face lit up upon seeing her. "Hey, Cassie, what're you doing here?"

She smiled and tried not to cry at the relief she felt. He was alive and talking, and his deep voice was the most wonderful sound in the world. He was pale, but at least it wasn't the ashen color she'd seen on him yesterday. "Hey, back at ya. I'm here to do your EKG. How are you feeling?"

"Good. Well, not really. I actually feel like I was in a submarine that imploded." His brow narrowed. "Didn't you work yesterday? I thought your Saturday and Sunday shifts were never on the same weekend."

As she pushed the portable machine into the space, Cass gestured to her jeans, cotton tee, and sandals. "Hence the reason I'm not in my usual scrubs. Since we're not related, I technically couldn't come into the CCU to see you, so I told the other cardiac tech, Tanya, I'd do your EKG for her this morning. There were a ton of orders waiting for her when she signed in, so she was more than happy to let me help out."

"I'm sure she was. But you should be home, relaxing on your day off. You look exhausted."

He hadn't meant it as an insult, and she didn't take it as one. It was a Dom thing. While he didn't love her, she knew he cared about her as a sub... and maybe as a friend. After all, they did know each other intimately. Cass also wouldn't admit he was right. She'd only had about three hours of sleep last night, or this morning as it were. She and Stefan's parents had left the hospital shortly after midnight since he hadn't woken up while they'd been there. Once back in her apartment, she'd tried to sleep, but it'd been elusive. All she'd been able to do was think about how close they'd all come to losing Stefan. She couldn't imagine a world without him in it. Cass wasn't exactly sure when she nodded off, but it'd been after 3:00 a.m., and then she'd been up with the sun a little over three hours later.

Instead of telling him all that, she smirked. "Well, I'm not the one lying in a CCU bed after having a major heart attack, so I *think* I'm looking a lot better than you right now. Or at least I hope I do."

Cass had spoken to his nurse, Nancy, before coming into

the cubicle and learned Dr. Chang had already seen Stefan and filled him in on everything that'd happened yesterday.

He snorted. "You always look better than me because you are, my little pixie."

Her heart skipped a beat at the endearment she hadn't heard in weeks and at the way he eyed her as if he were drinking her in and savoring every drop.

Not wanting to read too much into his words, she got busy plugging in the machine and getting the leads ready. Without her prompting, Stefan lowered the blanket and sheets to his abdomen and pulled the thin, blue gown he wore up to his chin, exposing his massive chest. Cass couldn't help but stare for a moment, her hand itching to touch him—and not in a professional manner.

Mentally shaking her head, she began to apply the leads in the proper places across his upper and lower chest. He hissed when her hand brushed against a short, bright-red streak on his upper right chest. "Sorry about that. You have some slight burn marks from the defibrillator paddles." She indicated a similar mark on the left side of his torso. "There's another one here. It happens a lot, but they don't look any worse than a sunburn."

Frowning, he inspected the areas. "I guess a few mild burns is better than the alternative."

She didn't even want to *think* of the alternative, which would've put him in the morgue instead of the CCU.

"You know," he said as she worked. "I don't get it. I'm under forty, eat healthy, keep my cholesterol down, exercise, don't drink much—how the hell did I end up having a freaking heart attack?"

Cass shrugged. "It's not always poor habits. Sometimes it's genetics, and sometimes it's just Mistress Nature being a bitch." She gave him a sassy grin. "So, Sir, what did you do to piss off the Mother of all Dommes?

A bark was followed by a chortle. "I honestly don't know, but I'd love to find out so I don't do it again. I need to get back on Mistress Nature's good side, I guess."

"Yes, you do. You can start practicing now. Stay still and be quiet for a moment."

"Yes, ma'am," he replied with a grin.

After pushing the start button, Cass waited for the printout to stop, then she hit the copy button for a duplicate she would leave at the nurses' station for Dr. Chang.

"That was a nice sound," she said softly as she removed the twelve leads from his chest.

His eyes narrowed. "What was?"

"Your laughter." Cass couldn't help it—her eyes welled up with tears.

She tried to turn away before he saw them, but Stefan grasped her elbow, stopping her momentum. "Hey, what's this?"

When she didn't look at him or say anything, he squeezed her arm. "Little pixie, please tell me those tears aren't for me."

Using her other hand, she wiped her eyes and cheeks. "I'm sorry, Sir—" She glanced at the partially-opened curtain. "I mean, Stefan. I was—I was just so scared when I heard there was a Code Ninety-Nine—a cardiac arrest—in the ER. Then when I got there and saw Ian, Mitch, and your captain and master chief, I knew it was you. I-I thought we lost you. I thought *I* lost you."

Those last words came out in a whisper, and for a brief second, Cass thought she'd kept them to herself. But when she finally met Stefan's intense gaze, she knew she hadn't.

"Aw, baby. Come here." He pulled her until she was sitting on the edge of the bed next to his hip, then he cupped her cheek. His thumb brushed a tear away. "I'm so sorry I scared you, Cassie, but I'm still here, and I'm going to be fine. The doctor said I'll be good as new in a few days. Don't cry, please."

Taking a shuddering breath, Cass nodded against his palm. "I'm okay. I'm just so happy you're going to be okay too." A noise outside the cubicle had her standing again. Even though today was her day off, it still wasn't professional for her to be sitting on his bed while she was there to do his EKG. "Um . . . oh, did your folks come to see you yet? They weren't in the waiting room when I walked by."

"My folks? Are here?"

"Mm-hmm. Captain Lowe called them, and they flew down on the first flight they could get. They got here around ten o'clock last night and spoke to Dr. Chang. Captain Lowe arranged for a hotel room for them up the street so they'd be close by. They were really tired when we left after midnight, so they probably slept a little late this morning. I'm sure they'll be here soon, but they can only come in for ten minutes at the top of the hour while you're in the CCU. Once you're in the step-down unit, they can stay all you want."

Stefan groaned. "Shit. Tell me they didn't call my sister."

Cass shook her head. "No. Your mom said Elin was in Italy with her girlfriend and planned on proposing the last night they were there, which I think is Wednesday. Your parents didn't want to interrupt their trip unless it was absolutely necessary. After finding out you came through the surgery okay, they agreed to wait until Elin got home to tell her."

"Thank God. Elin and Tara have been together for three years, and my sister has been planning this proposal for months. She was so nervous about everything, and the last thing I want her to have to do is postpone it."

"I know. Your mom told me all about it. I think it's romantic Elin's doing it at the Trevi Fountain."

A smile spread across his handsome face. "Yeah, it is.

Neither one of them had ever been to Italy, and it was on both their bucket lists, so Elin thought it would be the perfect place to propose."

They stared at each other for a moment, and Cass found she was suddenly at a loss for words. Before she could come up with another topic to talk about, just so she could stay with him a little longer, the curtain opened all the way. A big male orderly named Kelvin strode in, pushing a gurney. "Mr. Lundquist? Time for your MRI."

Cass took a step back. "Um . . . that's my cue to leave. If your parents are outside, I'll tell them you're going for the test."

"Thanks," Stefan replied. Then, before she could turn around, he added, "And Cassie?"

"Yeah?"

"Thanks for stopping by . . . and everything."

She gave him a small smile. "No problem. You just get better, you hear? That's an order."

"Yes, ma'am."

# Ten

Lying in the MRI tunnel, Stefan's back and head were killing him. His back because of the hard platform he was on, and his head because of the loud whirring and clanging noises the machine made as it took pictures of his heart, layer by layer. But neither pain was worse than the one in his gut. He couldn't stop thinking about Cassie crying over him. His damaged heart had clenched when he'd seen her tears. What he wouldn't give to take away her distress. His first thought on how to do that was to get his ropes and tie her up in a beautiful pattern until she couldn't move at all.

Unfortunately, that hadn't been an option for several reasons. One, he was in the hospital recovering from a freaking heart attack—*did I mention I'm only thirty-eight years old?* And two—he was no longer Cassie's Dom. That fact saddened him more today than it had in the past three weeks.

"Almost done, Mr. Lundquist," a voice said through a speaker in the wall.

Many people found the MRI tunnel brought out their claustrophobia—even if they hadn't been aware they'd had it before then—but it really didn't bother him. He'd just closed his eyes and tried to focus on something other than the noise and Cassie's tear-filled eyes, but his mind hadn't settled on anything better. Instead, it was something worse. His career was at stake. A heart attack, resulting in a cardiac arrest, would make him unfit for duty in the eyes of the US Coast Guard, no matter how well he recovered in the coming months.

He only had sixteen years in—four shy of what was needed for a full retirement. If he'd had at least eighteen years under his belt, the medical board could make a decision that would allow him to work light duty for the remaining time it would take to reach his full twenty. It wouldn't have been a guaranteed deal, but there was a limited exception rule in the policy for certain situations—not that it made a difference in Stefan's case. He was basically screwed, and it was pissing him off.

Since joining the USCG, all he'd ever wanted was to be a lifer. He'd planned to keep rising through the ranks, getting as high as he could before he hit the mandatory retirement age at sixty-two. Hell, he would've even been satisfied with retiring in his mid-fifties—between his pension and his trust fund, he would've been very comfortable. He'd still be financially secure with a disability pension and the trust, but being benched before reaching forty? Well, that seriously sucked. *Damn it!*

The clamor of the machine suddenly stopped, and a door opened somewhere behind the top of his head. "All done," the too-cheery female technician announced.

The platform moved, drawing him out of the tunnel. "How'd it look?"

"Sorry, I just run the test. The doctor will read the results and give them to you."

He should've expected that answer. It was basically the same one Cassie had given him . . . yesterday? Wow. It'd only been about twenty-four hours since they'd rescued the family of four, but it seemed like much longer than that to him.

Maybe his mind had altered his sense of time due to the fact he'd been clinically dead for a few minutes.

God, that gave him chills. There'd been no bright light, no seeing his grandparents on "the other side," no floating above his body and staring down at it, and no feeling of "I'm about to die." He didn't remember anything between the moment Cassie had left him lying on the gurney in the ER and the few minutes after he woke up this morning before meeting Nurse Nancy. The rest was an utter blank. One would think he'd remember getting hit with up to 360 electrical joules each time they'd shocked him with the defibrillator, but he didn't. The only proof he had that'd happened was the red first-degree burn marks on his chest and side. Well, that and everyone mentioning it.

Ten minutes later, with the help of Nurse Nancy and the burly orderly, who'd said his name was Kelvin, Stefan moved from the gurney back into his bed. It hadn't been the easiest thing to do since he was still hooked up to a bunch of wires and tubing, including that fucking catheter.

After Kelvin left the cubicle with the gurney, Stefan asked, "Nancy, is there any way we can get that—that thing . . ." He pointed to his groin, which was covered by the blanket and sheets again. ". . . taken out?"

She chuckled as she unhooked him from the portable heart monitor to the stationary one over his left shoulder. "I'm surprised you waited this long before asking me that. With most men, it's the first question out of their mouths as soon as they can talk. I'll page Dr. Chang—if he gives me the okay, I'll remove it. After that, you can use a urinal."

He didn't care what he had to piss in, he just wanted that damn thing out of his cock. It was . . . icky.

"Thanks."

"You're welcome. By the way, your parents are in the waiting room. I told them you were getting an MRI. They can visit at the top of the hour for ten minutes—I'll let them know you're back."

After thanking her again, he glanced at the clock as she left and partially closed his curtain. He had twelve minutes to kill before his parents could come in. Grabbing the TV remote, since there wasn't anything else he could do but sleep or stare up at the ceiling, he flipped through the thirty or so limited channels twice and finally settled on ESPN to get the scores and recaps of yesterday's games. However, when the curtain opened again and his parents entered, he couldn't recall a single score that'd flashed across the screen or even who'd played whom.

"Hi, honey." His mother leaned over the bedrail, kissed his cheek, and ran a hand over his crewcut like she used to do when he was a kid. "How are you feeling?"

"I'm good, Mom. Hey, Dad. You know you didn't have to rush down here—"

His father frowned as he circled to the opposite side of the bed from his wife and patted Stefan's shoulder. "Of course we did, son. We're just glad to see you're okay. We spoke to Dr. Chang, and he said your prognosis is good."

"Yeah, he told me that too." He refused to mention that prognosis didn't bode well for his career. Stefan gestured to the ugly recliner behind his father, the only seat in the small cubicle. "Mom, sit there. You both must be exhausted. Cassie said you were here until after midnight."

His mother smiled as she perched on the edge of the seat. "She's an absolute sweetheart. We tried to tell her it was okay to go home, but she insisted on staying until we left in case we needed anything."

There was no mistaking the twinkle in his mother's eyes, and Stefan rolled his own. "She's *just* a friend, Mom."

"A very pretty friend. I like her."

"So do I, but we're still *just* friends." Geez, he'd had an MI, gone into cardiac arrest, had surgery, was lying there hooked up to a bunch of wires, and had more tubes entering his body than he was comfortable with, and his mother was playing matchmaker. And why did it grate on his nerves trying to convince his mother Cassie and he were "just friends"? For ten months, they'd been so much more. He'd been her Dom, and she his submissive. They'd been intimate. In binding her within his Shibari patterns, he'd given Cassie what she needed, and in return, she'd given him her submission and pleasure.

But what did he really know about his little pixie beyond the basics? After his parents' ten minutes were up, he thought about what little he knew about Cassie and ticked the items off on his fingers, unfolding them one by one. She was twenty-nine years old, never married, and had no children to his knowledge. She worked as a cardiac rehab tech at the hospital he was currently laid up in and had gone back to school to become a nurse. She had an inexplicable need to be restrained in order to have an orgasm, something he'd been more than happy to help her with. She had a pretty smile, gorgeous hazel eyes, and a killer body. She . . . she . . . hmm.

Stefan stared at his hands. Nine up and one down. Was that all he knew about her? Less than how many fingers he had? Nine freaking things? There had to be more than that after ten months in a D/s relationship. He knew nothing about her family, whether her parents were still alive, and if she was close to them. He had no clue if she had any siblings. What did the inside of her apartment look like? Did she have a pet living with her? And what was the name of the perfume she always wore—the one that made him hard as soon as the scent reached out and tantalized his nose?

All he *did* know, besides the few things he'd listed above, was how to make her come and how beautiful it was when she did. Had he really distanced himself that much from her, even when his cock had been deep inside her? God, he was such an ass.

―――

Five minutes after Devon Sawyer and his wife, Kristen, left Stefan's room in the cardiac step-down unit, Master Chief Graves, Ensign Peters, and Ensign Jacoby strode in, and he stifled a groan. He knew his friends and coworkers meant well, but he really didn't want anyone seeing him in this impaired condition, aside from his parents.

The only person he was torn about visiting was Cassie. He didn't want her to see him at his worst, but she'd brightened his world every time she'd stopped in over the past two days. After he'd been moved out of the CCU late yesterday afternoon, she'd come by, bringing one of his very few unhealthy vices—a chocolate mint shake from Donovan's Pub. Somehow, Cassie had remembered the shake from the one time they'd ordered takeout from the bar/restaurant for dinner one night when Stefan hadn't been in the mood to cook before an evening of play at his place. He'd tried to brush off how good her gift had made him feel at the time, but a part of him was still pleased.

Cassie had also stopped in to see him that morning before her shift in the cardiac rehab unit started and again a little while ago on her lunch break, just before Dev and Kristen had walked in.

As the three men filled the room, Peters was the first to greet him. "Hey, LC, you're looking good."

Stefan snorted as he stretched his legs out under the blanket covering his lower body. "Don't lie to your superiors, Ensign—I know I look like crap."

He sure as hell *felt* like crap, so it was a given he looked like it too.

Two days after his heart attack and subsequent procedure, his muscles seemed to deteriorate with every passing hour. He was weaker than he could ever remember being, and he hated it. The muscles in his shoulders and chest were stiff and ached like someone had given him a severe beating a few days ago. Every time he lifted his arms or turned onto his sides, he was reminded of the burns from the defibrillator, which still marked his upper torso. He no longer had the oxygen cannula stuck in his nose, but the IV and monitors were still in place. At least the damn urine catheter had been removed from his dick, and thankfully, not by "Big Jim"—Nurse Nancy had taken care of it, and Stefan had blushed the entire time.

Stefan was hoping to get sprung from the hospital soon, but according to Dr. Chang, he'd be there until at least Wednesday. They were trying to get his blood pressure under control since it had been elevated over the past twenty-four hours, and he still had to take a nuclear stress test. He'd been told the MRI and an echocardiogram had shown mild damage to his heart muscle, but with rehab, it should improve. Unfortunately, it *didn't* improve his chances of staying with the Coast Guard. That was another reason he didn't want visitors —he wanted to wallow in self-pity for a while—but he couldn't be rude to the people who truly cared and were worried about him.

The three men chuckled as they took up positions around the private room, which was courtesy of Ian and Devon. Apparently, the Sawyer brothers made sizable donations to several hospitals in the Tampa/St. Pete area every year, and it came with benefits.

"The family we rescued from the downed plane," Graves started, "came by the air station to thank us today and brought a reporter and photographer with them. The higher-ups thought it would be good press to put our ugly mugs in the paper and on social media."

"What the hell were they thinking?" Stefan teased. "Did the camera break when they zoomed in on you, Peters?"

There was a round of laughter before Jacoby spoke up. "I'll admit, though, it felt really good to see those kids again." He unrolled a piece of paper Stefan hadn't realized the younger man had been carrying. "The little girl, Emma, gave this to me. I think I'll have it framed as a reminder of my first successful rescue in SAR."

In different colored crayons, she'd done her best to draw a helicopter, a life raft on water, and a bunch of stick figures, two of which were hanging on a rope.

Everyone smiled. Their rescues weren't always successes, but it was nice to have a reminder of the ones that were since the unsuccessful ones would unfailingly come to mind before all others for the rest of their lives.

"By the way . . ." Graves set a duffel bag on one of the two chairs in the room. "The nurses in the ER gave me your keys, wallet, and boots. The medics had to cut your jumpsuit off while you were unconscious."

Stefan's eyebrows shot up. It hadn't even occurred to him over the past two days to wonder where his stuff was. The master chief continued. "I drove your truck back to the townhouse and left it there. Then, I figured while I was there, I might as well grab you some clothes and stuff. There's three T-shirts, two pairs of sweatpants, socks, and sneakers in the bag, and a few things from your bathroom I thought you'd want. Also, I found your cell phone in the truck, so that's in there, too, with your keys and a charger. I didn't think you'd need your wallet for anything, and it was safer to leave it in the top drawer of your dresser instead of having it here, but I can get it if you need it."

"Thanks, Master Chief. You're right, I don't think I need my wallet, but I appreciate you taking care of everything else and bringing me some clothes. My ass is hanging out of this stupid hospital gown." And he planned on changing into a shirt and sweats as soon as his buddies left. Maybe he'd feel a little better being in his own clothing. He didn't think he could feel much worse.

"Could be worse—your dick could be hanging out." He paused a moment, and then his expression became somber. "Listen, LC, I didn't get a chance to properly thank you for saving my sorry ass out there. I-I thought I was a goner for a second there."

Stefan stared at the man, then let out a soft huff. "That's it? No case of scotch? No tickets to the Super Bowl? Shit, saving a buddy's life has gone downhill in the gratitude department lately, hasn't it?"

Everyone burst out laughing. They knew Stefan was no more comfortable with the thanks than any one of them would've been. They did what they could to save as many lives as possible for one reason only—because they could. The protection of life had been ingrained in all of them from the beginning, and that came first and foremost over everything else, including their own lives.

When Graves spoke again, despite the levity of the moment, his words were tinged with regret. "Well, I hope saving my ass wasn't what brought the heart attack on. I mean, you could've found out about the blockage in a way that was less severe."

Frowning, Stefan glared at him, his tone reproving. "Master Chief, I will never regret saving you. And if I ever hear you blaming yourself for my fucking heart attack, I'll beat the ever-loving daylights out of you, understood?"

The corners of the man's mouth ticked upward. "Aye, aye, Sir."

"Good. Now, who snuck in a flask of scotch? I know one of you did."

# Eleven

Cass glanced up when the door to the cardiac rehab unit opened, and she smiled. Kelvin pushed Stefan's wheelchair inside and stopped next to her elevated console in the middle of the large room. The orderly handed her a thick chart with all the patient's info in it. "He's all yours. Page me when he's ready to go back to his room."

"Thanks, Kelvin." As the big man left, Cass studied Stefan. The grin he gave her didn't quite reach his eyes. "It'll be a few minutes until Dewayne is available to get you set up. How're you feeling?"

"Fine."

She tried not to frown at the flat, one-word answer as he looked around the room. Cass's monitoring station was where she kept an eye on all the patients while their EKGs scrolled across her computer screen. Surrounding her, there were numerous pieces of gym equipment, which included treadmills, stationary bikes, ellipticals, rowers, a cross-country ski machine, and a Stairmaster. There was also a weightlifting area with dumbbells. Everything was used to strengthen one's heart muscle following any of a variety of cardiac episodes.

Several men and women, currently all outpatients, were scattered around the large room, doing their assigned exercises while wearing heart monitors. If Cass noticed any abnormalities in their EKGs, then she would notify one of the two cardiac rehab specialists who were working with the patients. Both Jane Tillman and Dewayne Reich had degrees in exercise physiology and helped nutritionist, Vivian Dickson, plan custom programs for their patients to follow. Most insurance companies paid for anywhere between three months and one year of therapy following a qualifying cardiac event.

Behind her station were men's and women's locker rooms, but since Stefan had come from upstairs, he didn't have anything that needed to go in there. Cass couldn't think of anything else to say to him, and he didn't seem like he was in the mood for any conversation, so she did her job and stared at the monitor.

Standing next to a recumbent bike, Dewayne took Mrs. Dobbs' blood pressure and called out the numbers for Cass to write down in the woman's chart. "One-eighty over eighty-four, Cass."

"Got it." After making the notation, Cass glanced at Stefan before watching the monitor again. He was frowning, and she didn't know why. She tried to look at the room from his perspective, and after a few seconds, she realized what he saw. All the other patients were over sixty-five years old and some were older than eighty. He had to be thinking he didn't belong with all these elderly people, but he was wrong. He needed the rehab as much as they did. He couldn't just throw himself back into the intense physical fitness routine he'd been doing before his heart attack. Whether he liked it or not, he was going to have to start back up slowly, and this room, where he could be monitored, was the best place for him to do that. He wasn't the youngest person they'd ever had in the hospital's cardiac rehab program, but he was currently.

After adjusting the tension on Mrs. Dobbs' bicycle, the male therapist strode over to Stefan and held out his hand. "Hey, man, ready to get started?"

Before the inpatients reported for their first workout session, either Jane or Dewayne visited them to explain the rehab program, and Cass knew the latter had stopped in to see Stefan yesterday afternoon.

Shaking the man's hand, while glancing around again, Stefan asked, "Is this really necessary? I mean, I work out practically every day at my station's gym and pool. I know how to use all this stuff already."

Bending down, Dewayne lifted the wheelchair's footrests out of the way, so Stefan could stand. "Like I told you yesterday, for the next few weeks, no exercise without an EKG monitor on. We've got to make sure the damage from the heart attack isn't causing any problems while it heals."

Stefan huffed as he stood. "Well, I could've at least walked down here on my own."

"No can do, man. Not while you're still an inpatient. Come on over here and let me hook you up to a monitor, so Cass can keep an eye on your EKG, and then we'll get you on the treadmill. No running today—just a stroll down the beach. Once your stress test is done, we'll see about getting you up to a jog and then running."

As Stefan followed the other man across the room, Cass could've sworn he'd mumbled a curse, but she wasn't sure. Instead, her attention was caught by Mr. Edwards singing along to Elvis Presley's "Jailhouse Rock" as it floated down from the overhead speakers, and it brought a smile back to Cass's face. Usually, they kept a light rock station on the satellite radio, since it appealed to several generations. However, if there were only a few patients in the room, the staff would take requests and switch to another genre if everyone agreed. Sometimes they had swing music on, and everyone got into it, dancing around the room. It was pretty fun to watch, and it got their heart rates up just as much as the aerobic equipment did.

Within a few minutes, a new EKG started scrolling across Cass's screen, and there was a pop-up request for her to enter the patient's name and identification number for heart monitor #8. From behind her, Dewayne asked, "Is Stefan up?"

"Yes, and he's in normal sinus rhythm at a rate of sixty," Cass replied as she used the keyboard to enter his information.

**Name: S-T-E-F-A-N L-U-N-D-Q-U-I-S-T**
**Patient ID: 20-549367-901**

After hitting "Accept," Cass clicked on the record button next to Stefan's EKG and printed out a ten-second strip for comparison for when they got his heart rate up.

Dewayne then rattled off Stefan's vital signs as he took them one by one.

"Blood pressure is one-forty over sixty-eight."

"Respirations, sixteen."

"Pulse, sixty-two."

"Oh-two sat is ninety-nine percent." That was the oxygen level in his blood.

"Temperature, ninety-eight point two."

Cass wrote each one down in the proper place on Stefan's assessment sheet. The last number was a little low, but a lot of people didn't have the "ideal" temp of 98.6 degrees. Checking his chart, she saw that it was normal for him.

After he was done taking Stefan's vitals, Dewayne escorted his patient to a treadmill within Cass's range of sight, even if her gaze was on the screen in front of her. If for any reason, she wasn't looking at the EKGs, and an abnormality occurred on one of them, like premature beats or an atypical high or low heart rate, an alarm would alert her to it. Since Cass oversaw the charts, answering the phone, and a few other things, it helped guarantee she wouldn't miss anything.

Over the next ten minutes, Cass did her job, but every so often her gaze would flitter toward Stefan. The big, bad Dom wasn't happy, and it was obvious. While Dewayne had set Stefan's treadmill at a faster pace than he would for the older patients, it was still only a walk. Stefan looked bored out of his mind and didn't like it when Jane returned his treadmill to a flat position after he'd elevated the incline without asking. He was trying to do too much on his first day, which wasn't uncommon with new patients, but the CRSs and Cass were keeping an eye on him, whether he liked it or not.

---

Stefan glared at the digital number showing his pace on the treadmill.

*My fucking grandmother could walk faster than this, and she's been dead for years.*

Yeah, he was being a surly bastard, but he was being treated like a ninety-two-year-old. First, his nurse and the big orderly wouldn't let him walk the hallway and take the elevator two floors down to the rehab unit. Nope, he'd had to sit in a wheelchair and be pushed the whole way. To add to his embarrassment, Cassie had seen him like that. Now, she was watching him walk a whopping 3.0 mph on the treadmill. He'd tried to increase the machine's incline to, at least, let him feel like he was actually doing some work, but the female therapist, Jane, had put it back down again.

What was pissing him off the most, though, was the whopping 3.0 mph, with no freaking incline, was starting to kick his ass. His heart rate was up as if he were running double the current speed, and he was sweating and getting out of breath. Not something that should be happening to him with such little effort. Hell, he could run the Trident Security obstacle course in under six minutes for Christ's sake, and that was based on the Navy SEALs' infamous O-course.

"How're you doing?" Dewayne asked as he checked the timer on the treadmill.

"Fine."

"Well, I know it feels like you're walking slower than a snail, but after what your heart just went through a few days ago, it's really getting a workout today. I see in your chart Dr. Chang ordered the stress test for tomorrow. After we get those results, we'll come up with a program to get you back to the workouts you're used to, within reason, of course. No obstacle courses or jumping out of helicopters or whatever else you guys do for fun in the Coast Guard. I can't say this enough, you can't push it, man. Let your heart heal. You wouldn't be running on a broken leg until it healed properly, so think of it that way. All right?"

In that regard, it kind of made sense, but that didn't make Stefan any happier about things. "Yeah, I get it. I'll try to take it easy for now."

"Good. Stick your hand out." When he did, the guy slid a sensor on his finger to get the O2 saturation in his blood. "It dropped a bit—ninety-five—but that's expected in the beginning."

Dewayne hit a red button on the treadmill, and the belt slowed before coming to a complete stop. "Take a breather, and I'll check it again in a minute. In the meantime, give me your arm."

A blood pressure cuff was wrapped around Stefan's upper arm and inflated. A few seconds later, Dewayne announced, "One-sixty-two over eighty. Not bad. Looks like the new blood pressure medication Dr. Chang put you on is working. That's good. Still have to keep an eye on it though because some meds can work too well and make you *hypotensive*. Definitely don't want that happening. If you get dizzy at all, lay down and elevate your legs."

Stefan nodded. He remembered all that from when he got his paramedic certification about ten years ago to become a rescue swimmer in SAR. He'd done that for nine years before his promotion about eighteen months ago moved him inside the Sector Command Center, where he oversaw the rescues instead of participating in them.

Dewayne ripped the blood pressure cuff off Stefan's arm. "What weights were you using for bicep curls?"

"Thirty for three reps."

"Well, we're going to cut that down to ten today. Yeah, yeah, I know—sissy stuff. I'll get you back to fifteen by next week. Baby steps, my man. Baby steps. We'll get you there."

*Baby steps, my ass.*

# Twelve

"I'm serious, Elin. I don't want you flying down here for nothing—you just got back from Italy and probably didn't even unpack yet. I don't need a babysitter, and I'm supposed to take it easy for a while, so we'd be sitting in the living room, staring at each other watching TV." He paced around said living room as he talked to her on his cell phone.

His sister tsked before saying, "You're a stubborn mule, little brother, but I'll leave you alone for a few weeks. But don't forget Tara and I are planning to come down for a long weekend next month, so you have until then to stop being so surly."

"I'm not surly." Even as he said the words, he knew she was right, and so did she.

"Sure you're not."

"I'm not." He didn't know why he continued to argue. "Anyway, let's talk about something else."

He sat in his recliner and stared out the bay window at nothing at all. He'd been home for just over two full days and only yesterday had finally convinced his folks to go home this morning. Thankfully, they'd managed to find a flight with seats available. He loved his folks, but having them hover over him like he was an invalid had been driving him crazy. Let them go fuss over the newly engaged couple. "So, how'd the proposal go?"

"It was amazing, Stef. I cried, Tara cried, a bunch of people around us cried. Somehow, I managed not to sound like a babbling idiot and got the words out. Tara was completely taken by surprise. I thought maybe she had an idea I might propose in Italy, but she says she never saw it coming."

"Glad to hear it, sis—you and Tara make a great couple. I'm happy for you. So, when's the wedding?"

"Don't know yet. We're trying to decide whether to do something small here with our family and a few friends or if we should just elope since Tara's family will refuse to come. I don't want that bothering her on the biggest day of our lives."

Stefan had heard all about his future sister-in-law's parents and other family members disowning her because she'd fallen in love with another woman. It still irked him that, in this day and age, people would do that to their own flesh and blood. It hadn't bothered him or his parents one bit when Elin announced she was a lesbian during her junior year of college. When she'd brought her first girlfriend home a year later for Thanksgiving, it'd all seemed so natural to seventeen-year-old Stefan. As long as his sister was happy, he didn't care which gender she was attracted to.

"Well, even if you elope, you'll need witnesses. I'm volunteering to be one. Just tell me where and when, and I'll be there."

"I'm holding you to that, little brother."

They chatted for a few more minutes before ending the call. While he loved being in Florida, he missed having his sister around. Despite the five-and-a-half years between them, they'd always been close. When he'd turned twenty-one, Elin had been the one to take him out for his first legal drink to celebrate. She also knew he was a Dom. He honestly didn't recall how that conversation had started a few years ago, but she hadn't treated him like a freak or a woman abuser—he was neither. In fact, while she wasn't in the lifestyle, she had two gay friends who were in a D/s relationship. So, by the time she found out Stefan was a Dom, she'd already known more about the lifestyle than he'd expected her to.

A thumping from outside had Stefan standing and looking down from the bay window. His street dead-ended two driveways down from his, and his neighbors had put up a basketball net for their sons and allowed any of the local kids to use it whenever they wanted. Even though there was an outdoor, full-sized basketball court on the other side of the complex, the half-court got a lot of use too. Right now, three of the teenage boys who lived on his street were shooting hoops.

As he watched them play, Stefan realized how bored he'd been all day. After he'd taken the stress test Wednesday morning, Dr. Chang had finally cleared him to be released from the hospital. Stefan had honestly thought he'd failed the damn thing since he'd gotten so out of breath and exhausted in a short amount of time as the pace of the treadmill had increased. But that cardiologist had assured him it had gone better than he'd expected.

Shortly after his parents had left for the airport this morning, Stefan returned to the hospital as an outpatient for his scheduled cardiac rehab session. The only thing that had made it bearable had been seeing his little pixie. Not that he'd let her know that—as his sister had said, he'd been surly. He was certain the therapists had wanted to tell him to suck it up and just do what they told him to without complaint. It was driving him nuts not being anywhere close to what he'd been able to do physically before his heart attack. On top of that, he had an appointment with a Coast Guard physician coming up on Tuesday. Although he'd been told it was a routine physical, he knew it was the first step toward his unwanted medical discharge.

*Fuck this shit.*

Pushing off the window frame, Stefan strode to the front door and walked outside. As he approached the three high school seniors, he called out, "Hey, how about a little two-on-two?"

"Hey, Stefan! Sounds great," Kenny Cooper replied. "You and me against Briggs and Sanders."

Tyrel Sanders tossed the ball to Stefan, who dribbled it a few times before passing it to Kenny while Marty Briggs tried to block him. Stefan cheered when his teammate's shot went through the hoop with nothing but net. Back and forth, they played on the half-court. After only a few minutes, though, Stefan started getting winded, but he wasn't giving up. There was no way he was getting sidelined by a fucking heart attack. It was only a pickup basketball game. What could it hurt?

Kenny caught a rebound and tossed it to Stefan. Without hesitation, he faked to one side, then brushed past Marty for a layup. As the shot bounced off the rim, Stefan crashed into Tyrel as they both reached for it. The two of them tumbled to the ground, and Stefan's head spun as he gasped for air.

―――

Cass steered her car into Stefan's neighborhood and slowed down under the speed limit since several kids were playing outside. As Cass was leaving work a little while ago, Stina Lundquist called her just to let her know she and John had flown home at Stefan's request. Stina knew her son didn't want them fussing over him now that he'd been discharged from the hospital, and while it was a mother's right to do so, she completely understood he needed some time to deal with everything. Knowing Stefan was surrounded by good and supportive friends made the decision to return to Connecticut easier for the couple. They'd also broken the news to Stefan's sister this morning after she and her now-fiancée had arrived back in the US.

After Stina had wished her well and then hung up, Cass had decided to pick up Stefan's favorites from Donovan's Pub and stop by for a visit since it was Friday and she didn't have any classes that evening. Yes, it was a little presumptuous of her to just show up with dinner for him, but he'd seemed so out of sorts in rehab that morning, and she wanted to do something nice for him. She just had to keep reminding herself not to let her heart get involved. This was just one friend helping out another friend—nothing more.

Turning down his street, she noticed some teenagers playing basketball at the dead end. Cass pulled into one of the visitor parking spots and climbed out of the car. When she turned to get the food out of the backseat, shouts caught her attention. She eyed the group of boys again and realized they weren't all teenagers. As she watched in horror, Stefan and one of the boys fell onto the ground, and Stefan grabbed his chest.

"Oh, my God!" Terrified, she ran toward them. "Stefan!"

Cass dropped to her knees beside him and clutched his hand. "Are you okay? Somebody call 9-1-1!"

"N-no," he rasped. "I-I'm okay, Ca—" A coughing fit cut off his words.

"No, you're not okay! You had a freaking heart attack not even a week ago! What the hell do you think you're doing?" Without waiting for an answer, she glared up at the three teenagers who were staring back at her as if her head was about to explode. "Why are you just standing there? Call 9-1-1!"

"Don't fucking call . . . 9-1-1," Stefan barked as he rolled onto his side and sat up. He was still trying to catch his breath, but it didn't appear he was struggling as much now. "I'm fine, Cassie. Just—just got the wind knocked out of me."

"Dude, is she kidding?" one of the boys asked. "You had a heart attack?"

Cass growled. "No, I'm not kidding, and yes, he had a heart attack last week. And he's not supposed to be doing anything strenuous, but he's too damn stubborn to listen to his doctor and therapists."

"Sorry, we didn't know," another boy said.

As Stefan slowly got to his feet, Cass stood and gave him a dirty look before turning to the boys and reining in her anger. "It's not your fault. Obviously, the stubborn mule didn't want you to know. Now that you do, if he tries to play any sports around here again without me telling you it's okay, you have my permission to tell him to bugger off."

As she eyed them, she realized that they were a little older than she'd first thought—young men, not boys. They grinned at her, and the tallest one said, "Stefan, dude, I like her, but you better watch your ass. She's not gonna take any crap from you."

"Damn right, I'm not."

When she scowled at Stefan again, she found him frowning at her. Her breath hitched, and her heart raced because she'd seen that look on his face many times before when he'd been in full-Dom mode. Well, poo on him because she was in health-care-giver mode, and she wasn't backing down.

She straightened her spine and crossed her arms. "We can discuss this out here with an audience, or we can go inside, and I can reheat the dinner I brought from Donovan's for you. What'll it be?"

# Thirteen

As he sat at the kitchen table, Stefan silently watched Cassie stomp around his kitchen, reheating the food she'd brought and setting up for their dinner. She'd informed him there was enough for both of them, and whether he liked it or not, she'd be eating with him because she was starving. At least she hadn't been so pissed off at him that she did what she'd threatened to do at one point—pour his chocolate mint shake down the drain. Although, every time she came close to the table, he clutched the tall takeout cup a little harder in case she got any ideas to take it away from him.

He realized this was the first time he'd ever seen her pissed off. Annoyed—yes. Angry—yes. Pissed off to the point he grew afraid every time she neared his butcher knives in case she decided to try and cut off his manhood—no, that was a first.

He had to admit, he'd almost laughed earlier when she'd called him a stubborn mule since his sister had used that exact wording not more than thirty minutes before that. But he'd seen the fear in Cassie's eyes before her outrage had taken over when she'd realized he wasn't having another heart attack.

Yeah, playing basketball with the teens and pushing himself past his current limits had been stupid, but he hadn't comprehended it until he'd heard Cassie's panicked voice yelling for someone to call 9-1-1. He'd scared the living daylights out of her.

Pushing back from the table, he stood and stepped in front of her when she turned back from the refrigerator with a butter container in her hand. She frowned and stared daggers at him. Yup, she was still at the pissed-off level. He'd hoped she would've brought it down a few notches by then.

He cupped her chin, praying she wouldn't bite his hand. "Cassie, I'm really sorry I frightened you."

He'd expected her to start railing at him again, so he was taken off guard when tears filled her eyes. She tried to pivot away from him, but he stopped her and pulled her into his arms. As she sobbed against his chest, soaking his shirt, he ran one hand down the back of her head while the other rubbed circles over her back. "Shh, little pixie. I'm so, so sorry. I was an idiot for pushing myself."

"Yes, you—you were," she mumbled into his chest.

As she tried to get her tears under control, Stefan just held her. How had he never noticed how perfectly her body conformed to his? The contours of her chest, abdomen, and hips fit against him like they were two connecting pieces of the same puzzle.

God, he shouldn't be thinking like that. Now, more than ever, he had nothing to give her. He could drop dead at any minute—hell, he'd already done it once—and his career status was up in the air. He mentally smacked himself in the head. Between his probable medical discharge, his savings, and his trust fund, he didn't need to work. But sitting home on his ass, playing video games, was not what he wanted to do with the rest of his life, no matter how much time he had left. He was just using that as an excuse to keep Cassie at a distance.

*Face the facts, you idiot. You're just no good at relationships.*

The two non-D/s relationships he'd had in college before becoming a Dom had ended in disaster. One of the women had even stalked him for months afterward, prompting him to file an order of protection against her. The other had tried to slander him and get him kicked out of school after he'd broken up with her and gone out on a date with a woman she'd disliked. Obviously, he'd made some poor choices in his youth.

Then a friend had taken him to a munch where he'd learned about the lifestyle. So many things had clicked into place for him after that. A Shibari demonstration he'd observed turned out to be the icing on the cake. Over the next few years, he'd immersed himself in the BDSM community and studied the art of sensual rope bondage from a Shibari Master.

While tying a sub up in his ropes was his favorite thing about being a Dom, the second-best things were the contracted end dates on any relationships he went into. At first, they hadn't mattered. He'd collared several subs and even a slave once without any concern for an end date or putting one into a contract. But when a few of those D/s relationships had ended as poorly as his non-D/s ones had, he'd no longer sign a contract without a specific end date—even if it was renewable each month. He made sure, going into the negotiations, the submissive knew their association would only be Dom/sub and not boyfriend/girlfriend. Since then, he'd never regretted a single one of those end dates... until now.

Pulling back, he lifted Cassie's chin until her gaze met his. Damn, she was so freaking pretty, and there was only one way to make her even prettier. "After dinner, would you like to play, little pixie?"

Her wet eyes darkened with desire, bringing his semi-erect cock up to full mast. But then her next words were the equivalent of throwing a bucket of ice-cold water on him. "No, Sir."

She shook her head, her gaze dropping to his chest. "I don't think we should. I-I really need to go home after we eat—I have a lot of studying to do for a test on Monday night. In fact, I'll just take my dinner home with me and eat it there while I study. I'm really not hungry right now."

That was complete and utter bullshit—at least the "not hungry" part of it. She'd told him only five minutes ago that she was starving. Normally, he'd call a sub out for lying to him —collared or not—and dispense a proper punishment, but he couldn't bring himself to do it right now. Cassie had taken time out of her evening to bring him his favorite foods and shake from Donovan's, and what had he done? Scared the shit out of her, made her cry, then tried to smooth it all over with an unspoken promise to tie her up in his ropes until she couldn't move before fucking her until she screamed his name.

*Shit. Light-bulb moment.* Sex was on his current no-strenuous activities list. The cardiologist had told him to avoid that particular deed for a few weeks—among plenty of others— until his second stress test, which was scheduled for next month. Cassie would probably know about that and most likely thought he was ignoring the doctor's orders again.

"We don't have to have sex, Cassie. Let me just practice and bring you pleasure." When she shook her head again, he scrambled to say something—anything to keep her from leaving him here alone. "Or, we could just eat and watch TV. You have all weekend to study. It was so nice of you to bring me dinner. The least I can do is share the meal with you. Then we can just hang out and find a movie to watch. That way, you can keep an eye on me and make sure I don't do anything else I'm not supposed to."

She didn't respond immediately, but her expression told him she was starting to waiver, so he brought out the big guns. "Please, my little pixie? I'll even let you choose the movie. You can pick the corniest chick-flick there is, and I won't complain about it one bit."

At least he wouldn't verbally, but in his mind, he might rattle off a few terms of disgust.

Taking a deep breath, Cassie let it out slowly as Stefan held his own. "Okay. I'll stay." She pointed a finger at him. "But just for dinner and a movie. No scening or anything else that's off-limits to you until your next stress test."

The smile that spread across his face was the biggest and most heartfelt he'd had since landing in the hospital. "Deal."

# Fourteen

***Twenty months ago . . .***

"Hey, Cassandra."

Putting a tray of dirty, empty glasses and water bottles she'd collected from several tables onto the bar, she glanced up at the bartender. He was one of the Doms she'd avoided playing with. Something about him made her uncomfortable, but at least he wasn't pushy like a few of them could be after she'd repeatedly turned them down. As a coworker and bartender, though, he was a nice enough guy. Cass was just picky about who she scened with. "Yes, Master Dennis?"

The tall man, dressed in black leather pants and a maroon T-shirt, handed her two cold bottles of water. "I know your shift is just about over, but please take these to Sasha. She called over here to say, and I quote, 'I'm dying of thirst, Sir.'"

Cass chuckled. "That sounds like her. I'll bring them to her and put her out of her misery, Sir."

"Thanks. After that, Master Ian wants you to find him down in the pit."

"Okay, Sir. Thank you." She wondered what the Dom-in-residence wanted with her. It wasn't to play since he was now happily engaged to his beautiful sub, Angie Beckett, and neither was into having a third in any of their scenes.

Hurrying to the other side of the oval balcony, which looked down over the first-floor "pit" where many BDSM scenes were being played out, she headed toward the club's small fetish boutique. It was a Saturday night at The Covenant and busier than usual for some reason. She'd been running almost nonstop during her four-hour waitressing shift. Thankfully, she got a ten-minute break every forty minutes.

Entering the shop, she smiled when Sasha greeted her with her palms up and her fingers wiggling in a "gimme" motion. "I'm dying here, girl!"

"So I've heard."

Sasha took one of the bottles, cracked it open, and chugged a quarter of it. "Ahhhhh. Thank you!"

"Where's the refillable bottle you always bring?"

"Accidentally left it in the locker room, and it's been too busy to go down and get it. This is the first time in over two hours that I've been alone for more than five minutes. We got in a shipment of lingerie from a new high-end designer and another one with some interesting toys yesterday, and it seemed like *everyone* wanted to take a look. They obviously liked what they saw because Master Mitch already needs to reorder a few things."

After putting the two bottles on a shelf under the register, she stepped out from behind the counter. "And oh-em-gee! You *have* to see what Master Ian bought for Angie. She's going to look gorgeous in it. I'm so damn jealous of that girl because she looks amazing in practically anything, but she's too freaking nice for me to hold it against her."

Selecting a hanger from one of the racks, she held up a

shiny gold bra and thong set with a matching collar and wristlets. A sheer, purple harem skirt completed the ensemble. "Tell me this isn't sexy as fuck! Master Ian has amazing taste to go with his lingerie fetish. I swear he's in here at least three or four times a month, and that's in addition to the stuff Angie says he orders online. She's got to have a separate closet just for her lingerie."

"I wouldn't be surprised. Speaking of Master Ian, though, I have to run. He wanted to see me after my shift."

"Mm-hmm."

The twinkle in her curvy friend's eyes and the humor in her tone said she knew something Cass didn't. Folding her arms, Cass glared at her. "All right, spill it, girl, and make it quick."

Sasha shrugged nonchalantly as she neatened the racks of sexy lingerie. "It's nothing, really. I just might've . . . sorta . . . kinda overheard Master Ian telling Master Ben he was going to introduce you to Master Stefan tonight and negotiate a Shibari scene for you on the big stage."

Cass's eyes bugged out. "Seriously?"

Master Stefan was a hunk of the highest order, and on top of that, he was a Shibari Master—right up her alley. He'd joined The Covenant last month, but Cass had only seen him there a few times, and she'd either been working or had already negotiated to play with another Dom. She'd also never had an opportunity to speak to him or watch him scene yet.

She'd heard through the submissive rumor mill he was in the Coast Guard, which she could totally see with his amazing, lean, and muscular physique and salt-and-pepper crewcut. Some guys looked much older when they started going gray, but Master Stefan was in his mid-thirties, and all the touch of gray did for him was make him even hotter, in her opinion. He totally rocked it.

"Of course, seriously! I wouldn't tease you about that. I

just hope he's not in a hurry to tie you up. I've got twenty minutes left before I can close up the shop and get down to the pit to watch."

Walking backward toward the door, Cass pointed at Sasha. "I'll try to slow things down a bit, but not so much that it pisses him off. I'm not in the mood for a punishment. But I'll do what I can for you."

Sasha grinned. "Awesome, girlfriend. You're the best. Have fun!"

If she was going to be tied up in a Shibari Master's ropes, she *would* be having fun and, hopefully, a few orgasms to go with it.

Striding quickly toward the club's elegant grand staircase, Cass wondered if she had time to head to the ladies' locker room first to fix her hair and makeup. She glanced at the watch she always wore while waitressing and decided she couldn't make the detour—Master Ian would be waiting for her, knowing full well her shift had ended a few minutes ago.

As she descended the staircase, she removed her gold and red bowtie, which would let the members know she was now off duty, so they wouldn't be asking her to fetch their drinks. Cass scanned the crowd. Roped-off scene areas filled the outer perimeter of the cavernous room under the second-floor balcony. Meanwhile, the middle contained numerous seating areas, some of which were set up like living rooms with couches, wingback chairs, coffee and end tables, with elegant lamps providing soft light, while pub tables and stools were scattered among them. On the floor, throw pillows were available for subs to kneel or sit on next to their Masters.

Half across the width and three-quarters across the length of the room was a stage that was usually reserved for demonstrations and collaring ceremonies only. A St. Andrew's cross had been pushed to the back of the platform, out of the way, and a heavy chain had been lowered from the ceiling. At the end of it, a suspension ring had been securely attached with a large carabiner hook. It appeared Master Stefan's scene was going to be the highlight of the evening, with his sub dangling in midair. Cass hoped that sub was her—she loved being enveloped in Shibari ropes.

Over the heads of the other members, Cass spotted Masters Ian, Mitch, and Stefan in front of the stage, talking. When she reached the bottom of the staircase, she weaved through the crowd and made her way toward them. As she approached, she forced herself not to ogle Master Stefan. While the two co-owners of the club were just as handsome, she'd known them for the past few years, so she was used to seeing them. Master Stefan, however, was the new McHottie, and her eyes hadn't gotten their fill of him yet.

When Cass was certain there was nothing or no one between the trio and her that she might trip on or bump into, she lowered her gaze to the floor. Stopping next to Master Ian, she went down on her knees, bowed her head, and placed her hands palms up on her thighs, then waited to be acknowledged. On his other side, Angie was in the same position, but a pillow cushioned her knees.

After a few moments, Master Ian's voice rumbled as he set a hand on her head. "Hello, Cassandra. Please stand—eyes on me."

"Yes, Sir." She got to her feet again, then lifted her chin until her gaze met his startling blue one. "You sent for me, Sir?"

"I did. I'd like to introduce you to someone. Master Stefan, this is Cassandra." Master Ian nodded his head in the other man's direction, giving her permission to greet him.

Cass's mouth watered as she got her very first closeup view of Master Stefan. God, he was gorgeous. He was wearing black leather pants and a heather gray T-shirt. Both were molded to his body in sheer perfection, and she had to swallow hard before she could speak. "Good evening, Sir. It's a pleasure to meet you."

Taking her hand, Stefan brought it to his lips and lightly kissed the back of her knuckles. "The pleasure is all mine, little pixie."

She practically melted into a puddle at the combination of his striking mahogany eyes, gorgeous face, broad shoulders and chest, deep voice, sweet gesture, and words. Her girly parts were on full alert, and she prayed Sasha hadn't misheard Master Ian earlier because she really, *really* wanted to scene with this stunning example of masculinity.

Somehow, when he released her hand, she managed to remember to greet the third man in the group, even though she'd already done so at the start of her shift. Turning to face Master Mitch, she said, "And good evening to you, again, Sir."

The club's co-owner/manager smiled at her before his cousin's voice demanded her focus again. "Cassandra, Master Stefan has offered to demonstrate a Shibari design on the center stage tonight, and he needs a submissive for it. Would you be interested?"

Keeping her gaze on Master Ian, she nodded politely, but inside, her body was doing an elaborate happy dance. "Yes, Sir, I would."

"I've given him a copy of your limit list. Has anything on it changed recently?" Every submissive's limit list was kept in files at the reception desk in the lobby of the club's entrance. Doms could research a sub's hard and soft limits before negotiating a scene with them. It made things easier on the Doms who were looking for a sub with comparable likes and dislikes regarding the many different types of BDSM play.

"No, Sir. It's up-to-date."

"Suspension play?"

"That's still a green limit for me, Sir." He knew that, but he would verbally cover everything, so there would be no misunderstandings between her and Master Stefan after the scene started.

"Public nudity and orgasm?"

A few years ago, Cass would've blushed and stuttered after being asked that question, but she'd had many orgasms out here in the pit ever since Master Ian had broken through her barriers and given Cass her very first one. "Those are also green limits for me, Sir.

"Any questions or concerns?"

"No, Sir."

"Then tell Master Stefan your safeword, please."

She swiveled her head to face the Dom she'd be scening with tonight. "I use the club's safeword, Sir. Red."

"Very good," he responded. "Red it is."

Master Ian put his hand on her shoulder and squeezed gently, drawing her attention back to him. "We're all looking forward to the scene, little one." He winked. "Enjoy it."

Cass couldn't suppress her giggle. Of course, the man knew her well after all this time. "I'm sure I will, Sir. Thank you."

"That goes for you too, Master Stefan."

The other Dom gave him a smile and a single nod in response.

As Master Ian stepped away, Master Mitch held out his hand to Cass. "I'll hold onto your watch and tie for you."

"Thank you, Sir. If you'd like, you can give them to Sasha when she comes down after closing the shop." She passed over the tie she was still holding, then removed her watch and gave that to him as well.

When it was only the two of them left standing there, Master Stefan lifted his open hand toward her in a silent request, and she placed her smaller one in it. Cass tried to ignore the tingling traveling up her arm and the anticipation of what was to come, but it was hard to. He had a working man's hands, calloused but not dry. She couldn't wait to feel them touching her all over.

"I have a few more things I'd like to discuss before we start," he said. "Does everyone call you Cassandra, or do some shorten it?"

"Most people call me Cassandra or Cass, Sir, but I'll also respond to Cassie. Just, please, don't call me Sandra, Sir. I don't care for that name."

His eyebrows went up a smidgeon. "Is there a reason why?"

She knew it was going to sound petty coming out of her mouth, but she'd learned to be honest at all times with a Dom. "There was a girl name Sandra in my high school, and we didn't get along, Sir. In fact, we despised each other, so when I hear that name, all I think about is her. I know it's kind of silly, especially since I haven't seen her since we graduated, but . . ."

He grinned at her, and her heart almost stopped when his dimples appeared. "Well, then, it's a good thing I can't see you as a Sandra. If you don't mind, I prefer Cassie. It's pretty, and it suits you."

Yeah, that melting feeling was back. "Cassie is fine, Sir."

"Cassie it is, then. Next, do you have any current or past physical injuries or conditions that might affect your flexibility or cause you pain while restrained and suspended?"

"No, Sir."

"Claustrophobia?"

"No, Sir."

"Good. Let me see your hands." When she held them out, he inspected their color and temperature, so he would notice any changes later that might result from her circulation being cut off. Letting go of her hands, he squatted down and did the same to her feet, then stood again. "Now, one more thing. While I'm more than happy to give you some orgasms after I have you all tied up, there will be no sex between us tonight—

that's not something I care to perform on the center stage, and I also plan on putting you deep into subspace. However, maybe some other night, we'll be able to scene in one of the public stations or private playrooms."

"I'd like that very much, Sir."

"So would I. But let me make myself perfectly clear, Cassie. Since I'm new to the club and the Tampa area, I have no intention of signing a contract or collaring a sub at this time. I will be playing with other subs after tonight. Occasionally, I may ask you to play again, but do not expect anything more than that from me. Understood?"

His intense gaze said he'd meant every word. While she was a little disappointed he wasn't interested in getting to know her better, she was fine with it. Non-relationship sex was common in the lifestyle, and she'd experienced it many times before. Besides, it wasn't like she knew anything about him, other than what she'd heard through the rumor mill—he could be a jackass for all she knew—but for some reason, Cass felt drawn to him. Maybe, over time, things would change, but for now, she said, "Yes, Sir. I understand completely."

"Do you have any questions for me?"

She couldn't think of any—Master Ian had been thorough. "No, Sir."

"Good. Then let's begin."

# Fifteen

With the little pixie's hand in his, Stefan led her up the few steps onto the stage. It'd been about two months since he'd done a rope scene with a submissive—between packing, moving to Tampa, and unpacking—but he could do one blindfolded. He'd apprenticed under several Shibari Masters over the years since first discovering the bondage art. Stefan had never known the true meaning of passion before falling in love with seeing a submissive swathed in his ropes, then running his fingertips over the temporary impressions they left on the skin after being removed. To him, it was the most sensual feeling in the world.

He guided Cassie to the center of the stage, where he'd already placed a large, square throw pillow on top of a gym mat. Directing her so her back was to the growing audience, he said, "Strip completely, little pixie, then kneel and fold your clothes neatly, placing them on the floor in front of you. When you're done, present for me exactly as you did for Master Ian. From this point on, you will only speak when I ask you a question or to say your safeword. Understood?"

"Yes, Sir. I do have one question I just thought of, though, Sir."

He stepped around the pillow to face her. "Eyes on me, Cassie." When she complied, he said, "I'm listening."

"Will you use a blindfold, earplugs or earphones, or a ball gag on me, Sir?"

Stefan studied her face for a moment. Damn, she was gorgeous. How had he not yet noticed her in the club the few times he'd been there? Surely, she would've garnered his attention if he'd seen her.

"Are any of those a hard limit for you?" They hadn't been on her list, but he wanted to ensure they weren't suddenly an issue.

"No, Sir, although I'm not fond of gags. I was just curious, Sir."

The corners of his mouth ticked upward. "Curious is good, Cassie. However, I won't tell you my plans for the scene beforehand other than you'll be suspended at some point. Safety is my number one priority for the subs I scene with, so I'm asking you to place your full trust in me that you won't be harmed. Aside from that, expect the unexpected."

She smiled at him, and his dick twitched. "If you've earned Master Ian's trust, then you also have mine, Sir."

Reaching out, he tucked a strand of her hair behind her ear. When she licked her lips, his gaze followed her tongue. It was a shame he'd already told her there would be no sex involved in their scene tonight because he would love to have those lips and tongue on his cock, which was now semi-hard. To ward off a full erection, he tore his gaze from her mouth and refocused on her hazel eyes. There was a combination of lust, anticipation, and faith—just what he'd wanted to see.

"Thank you for that, Cassie. Do you have any more questions?"

She shook her head. "No, Sir."

Taking a step back, he pointed at the pillow between them. "Then begin."

Leaving her to follow his orders, Stefan stepped over to a small table where he'd already laid out his equipment and ropes. Earlier, when the chain with the suspension ring had been lowered from the ceiling, he'd scaled and hung from it with his full weight to ensure his submissive wouldn't be in danger of falling. He was sure the Sawyers took the welfare of their club members seriously, but Stefan was not one who just assumed equipment was safe because someone told him it was.

Picking up a small microphone Mitch had given him, Stefan clipped it to the collar of his T-shirt. As if on cue, someone lowered the club's music until it was barely background noise. He tapped the mic and was satisfied when the sound came through loud and clear over the speakers.

Strolling back and forth along the front of the stage, he greeted the crowd that'd gathered to watch. "Good evening, everyone. For those of you who don't know me, I'm Master Stefan, and although I'm new to The Covenant, I've been a Shibari Master for many years. The club's owners have asked me to give a demonstration tonight, and I thank them for the opportunity to show off what has become my passion.

"As with all BDSM play, please don't try anything you see tonight without proper training. It's taken me years of working with other Shibari Masters to get to the skill level I'm at now. Remember, Shibari is edge play because it entails the risk of very serious injury or death, especially if it's not done properly. While I take considerable care in making sure my submissive is safe, there's always a chance something can go wrong.

"Tonight will be an exhibition demonstration, which means you'll hear me talking to my submissive and an assistant only. I won't be speaking to you, the audience, as I would be during a training demo. However, if you have questions for me later, I'll be more than happy to answer them once I've given my submissive the proper aftercare. I expect she'll be deep into subspace before I finish the scene. I don't mind if the scenes around us continue, but please do not approach the stage and distract me or my sub, especially while I have her suspended. Thank you."

With his spiel over, he left the microphone on, so they could hear him talk to Cassie, and returned to his equipment. Grabbing a flat-edged scissor, he tucked it in his back pocket in case he had to quickly cut down the sub in an emergency. He then picked up a hair tie and rolled it onto his wrist before selecting a hair clip and attaching it to the front pocket of his leathers.

When he spun around to face Cassie, he was pleased to see she'd followed his instructions to the letter. She was on her knees, palms up on her thighs, her pale ass cheeks resting on her heels. Her head was bowed in submission, and her long hair draped downward, partially covering her face. Completely nude, she looked stunning—like an ancient goddess or a forest nymph.

Stefan strode over and turned his back to the audience as he stood behind her and straddled her hips. "Just putting this gorgeous hair up, little pixie, so it's out of my way."

He liked how she hadn't given him a response since he hadn't asked a question. Ian had told him Cassie's past training, obedience, and willingness to please would make her the perfect submissive for tonight's demonstration. Stefan was starting to see how true that was. The Dom-in-residence had chosen well for him.

Gently running his hands through the silky strands, he drew them all up and back behind her head, making sure he hadn't missed any, then used the tie to create a ponytail. He wrapped the tail around its base, forming a bun, which he then clipped into place.

Circling to her front, Stefan held out his hand. "Stand, subbie. Present position with your arms behind your back. Grab your forearms near your elbows."

Placing her hand in his, Cassie gracefully rose to her feet, then spread them shoulder-width apart. She clasped her arms behind her back and kept her head bowed. Bending, Stefan placed her neatly folded skirt and bra on the pillow, then picked up the pile. He set them far off to the side, where he wouldn't trip over them.

A smaller chain hung from the rafters, where it was connected to the heavier one through a series of pulleys. He adjusted them so the suspension ring was even with Cassie's hip, about three feet away from her, then secured the smaller chain to a hardpoint—an eyebolt—mounted on the floor at the edge of the stage.

Ignoring the audience and the sounds of play still taking place along the outer perimeter of the room, he returned to the table and selected several lengths of the soft jute rope he used. Each one had been handmade in Japan, specifically for the art of Shibari.

Stefan laid the ropes out on the stage near Cassie, where they'd be within his reach. Someone once asked him why he just didn't keep the table holding the ropes close by. He had responded that moving it out of the way later so he could suspend his sub tended to interrupt his momentum and bring him out of his Dom space.

Off to the side of the stage, Marco DeAngelis stood with his arms crossed, waiting for Stefan's signal. For the design he planned to do tonight, Cassie didn't need to be lying down while he worked. Each rope he used would be positioned in a certain way and attached to the suspension ring hooked to the chain dangling from the ceiling. Once he had her all set, Master Marco would support Cassie's tilting body as Stefan pulled on a smaller chain that would elevate her until she was lying horizontally four feet off the ground. If Cassie started going deep into subspace before then, Stefan would have Marco lend a hand by supporting her if she began to sway.

In the past, Stefan had seen more than one sub go too deep before he'd finished tying them up, and they'd nearly crashed to the floor. After the first time, when he'd, luckily, scooped the woman up before she fell, he always had another Dom nearby if he was working on a standing sub. When they were kneeling, sitting, or supine, it didn't matter since he would have them either on a massage table or a large padded mat on the floor.

After selecting his first rope, he slowly circled the naked sub, taking in every inch of her creamy skin from head to toe. She had tan lines from a strapless, string, two-piece bathing suit. Next time he played with her, he'd make her a bikini out of his ropes—one that squeezed her breasts and had a knot that sat right over her clit.

Stefan ran a finger from her bent elbow, up her arm, and across her chest, stopping to flick each nipple, which tightened. He was blessed with a sharp hitch of her breath.

"You're very pretty, my little pixie. I can't wait to see how exquisite you make my ropes." No, he hadn't reversed his words by accident. It wasn't his ropes that made his designs so gorgeous and mesmerizing—it was the subs who submitted to him and allowed themselves to be restrained. He thought the same thing about women's fashion. It wasn't the clothes that made a woman beautiful—it was the woman who made them look beautiful. When a woman had the confidence to own any room she walked into, that was one of the sexiest things in the world to him. Of course, there was a difference between cocky and confident.

Rounding to her back, he tied her forearms together without letting the rope wrap around either wrist. He wouldn't attach this rope to the harness he would create on her upper torso to avoid the risk of damaging the nerves in her arms. Once her arms were secured, he selected another rope to start on the harness. As he worked, braiding, tucking, twisting, and knotting, he continually checked to make sure the ropes weren't too tight so as to damage her skin or cut off the circulation.

Within moments, Stefan was in his zone—the one where everyone else disappeared except the sensual submissive, who was on the edge of euphoria. The rope went around her upper arms twice, crisscrossing over her chest before he brought it up and over her shoulders. He then weaved an intricate knot along her spine. The ropes were placed strategically, some of which would be connection points to the suspension ring, which would support the main load of the sub's weight when she was lifted off the ground.

Slowly but efficiently, he maneuvered the rope around her upper torso. When he reached the end of one, he tied it off and started with another. Every so often, he would bring the working end of the rope out and through the suspension ring, knotting it and leaving some slack for later when he began to lift her. Another rope was threaded through the lines between Cassie and the ring. Using bridge knots added extra support while keeping the other ropes at the proper distance from each other.

"How're you doing, little pixie?" he asked when he faced her again, wrapping the jute around her hips. "Open your eyes and give me a color."

"Green, Sir." Her voice was soft and dreamy, and her eyes were dilated. Yup, she was going under nicely.

"Good girl. Please let me know if you are feeling dizzy, can't breathe easily, or if anything hurts."

"Yes, Sir. Right now, I don't have any dizziness, trouble breathing, or pain." He liked how she repeated each one back to him, so there were no misunderstandings. "I'm a little light-headed, but nothing that hasn't happened when I've been restrained before. It's the start of subspace for me."

Stefan grinned and flicked her nipple, eliciting a moan from her before he continued. Dropping to his knees, he wrapped and knotted the rope around one thigh, below the point where it could pinch the femoral artery, and then brought the working end up and tied it to the suspension ring. He did the same thing above her knee with another rope. After he checked her circulation, he slid his hands down to her lower calf, where he repeated the process one more time a few inches above her ankle.

Turning his head, he gestured for Marco to join them in the middle of the stage. When the Dom stopped next to Cassie, Stefan instructed, "Just hold her upper arm, in case she sways . . . good." He gently tapped the sub's leg, the one furthest from the suspension ring. "Cassie, bend your knee and put the sole of your foot against your other leg."

After ensuring Marco was keeping her well balanced, Stefan tied a rope around Cassie's other calf, then secured it to the ring. Starting at her lower legs, Stefan inspected every knot, every twist, and every line his ropes made. He double-checked Cassie's circulation and the rigging attached to the ring.

Once he was certain everything was in order, he addressed Marco. "Place one hand behind her neck and the other on the front of her shoulder. As I pull her feet off the floor, maintain just enough pressure to keep her from spinning forward or backward until she's fully horizontal. As she rises, move the hand on her shoulder to the side of her head. I'll then set her head lower than the rest of her, so there's no strain on her neck and shoulders."

"Got it."

Once Stefan had her suspended, he'd only have a maximum of twenty minutes to get her off and for the audience to admire his work. Any longer, and he risked giving her nerve damage.

He turned back to Cassie. "How are you, little pixie? Give me a color."

She cracked open her eyes, and he could see she was in subspace. A dreamy look filled her beautiful face, and it was difficult for her to keep her heavy eyelids up. She was basically drunk on the endorphins coursing through her body. "Still green, Sir. No pain, tingling, or dizziness."

"Good girl. Are you ready to fly?"

Her eyelids fell again. "Yes, Sir."

*Perfect.*

Stepping over to the edge of the stage, Stefan unhooked the smaller chain from the hardpoint, holding it so the suspension ring on the other chain didn't drop to the floor. Slowly, hand over hand, he pulled on the chain connected to the pulley system, and the ring Cassie was attached to began to ascend. When the lines between her and the ring grew taut, she began to rise with them. Her body went lax as Marco supported her head and neck. Her one knee remained bent as her thighs spread a little more. She looked stunning as he lifted her higher and higher. With the shorter ropes attached to her legs, they became elevated a few inches above her upper torso, tilting her head downward. When she was about four feet off the ground, he hooked the chain to the hardpoint again, ensuring it was secure.

He strode toward her and nodded at Marco. "You can let go now."

The man removed his hands and stepped back to the side of the stage again. He'd remain there for the rest of the scene in case of an emergency.

Stefan circled Cassie, rechecking all the knots, connection points, and her circulation. Her hands and feet were still a good color and temperature. He could smell her arousal, which had increased while he'd worked the ropes around her.

Pushing on her shoulder, he slowly spun her around for the audience to see. Faint murmurs of appreciation reached his ears as the club members fixated on Cassie. Her eyes remained shut with a look of pure contentment on her face.

She was an amazing submissive, one of the best he'd ever scened with. For being such a good girl, now came her ultimate reward. His hand went between her legs, where she was warm, wet, and completely bare for him. He toyed with her clit, drawing a sexy gasp and moan from her. She couldn't move and was completely at his mercy. If time weren't a factor, he'd play with her like this all night.

Sliding the fingers of his other hand into her pussy, he enjoyed the heat he found. Her walls were already rippling, anticipating the climax that was so close. She was so turned on it would only take a few moments to have her coming. "I want to hear you scream for me, little pixie. I want them to hear you taking your pleasure all the way out in the parking lot."

"Oh, God! Yes, Sir! Please!" Her breathy voice made him hard as a rock, and once more, he regretted not being able to fuck her with his cock right now.

He began to plunge his fingers in and out of her, repeatedly, while torturing her swollen clit. Her breathing increased, as well as her moaning and begging. Knowing he was running out of time, he searched for and found her G-spot, pressing on it and her clit simultaneously. She clenched around his fingers and exploded, wailing with her release for all to hear.

When her body sagged against the ropes, Stefan reluctantly withdrew from her core. Unable to help himself, he licked his fingers clean. She tasted delicious. This sub was one he was definitely going to have to play with again for so many reasons, and next time, his cock would be inside her when she came.

Returning to the edge of the stage, he unhooked the chain and slowly lowered her body to the mat on the floor. As he was striding back to her, so he could start removing the ropes, the audience broke out in applause. He hoped it was in response to his beautiful sub instead of his rope work because she deserved all the credit in this scene.

Stefan knelt beside Cassie and studied her face, seeing nothing but utter bliss. When he reverently stroked her cheek, she opened her eyes halfway, smiled at him, and whispered, "Thank you, Sir, that was wonderful."

"Yes, my little pixie. It most certainly was."

# Sixteen

*Present . . .*

At 1300 hours, Stefan knocked on Captain Lowe's office door at USCG Sector St. Petersburg and waited for permission to enter. When it was granted, he pushed the door open and walked in before halting, tucking the small box he was carrying under his left arm. He stood stiffly at attention and brought his right hand up to his temple to salute his superior officer. "Lieutenant Commander Lundquist reporting as ordered, sir."

"At ease, LC," Lowe said before Stefan had barely finished his greeting. The older man gestured to the door, not bothering to rise from behind his desk. "Close the door and have a seat."

Okay, so this would be at least a somewhat informal yet closed-door meeting. Under the circumstances, that wasn't a good thing, in Stefan's opinion. It had been three weeks since his heart attack and four days since his appointment with Commander Harrison, a physician with the Medical Evaluation Board. Stefan was pretty sure he was looking at the end of his career with the Coast Guard, but a small part of him was holding onto a thread of hope. After his exam, the commander hadn't told Stefan what his decision would be, stating he had to review all the medical records and test results from the hospital before making his final recommendation to the board.

Taking one of the two guest chairs in front of the desk, Stefan set the box on the other one and waited for the captain to continue. The man leaned back in his luxurious, leather executive chair and eyed him. "How're you feeling?"

"Great, sir," he lied. "The rehab therapists are getting me back to where I was before. Should be—"

His eyes narrowing, Lowe held up a hand, stopping him. "Commander, I want the fucking truth. Not some bullshit you've been spouting to everyone else. We've known each other a long time now—don't try to snow me."

It was true. Lowe had been Stefan's commander at Air Station Atlantic City in New Jersey before being promoted to captain and transferred to Florida. Two years later, Stefan had been promoted to Lieutenant and transferred to Air Station Clearwater, where he was once more under Lowe's command. Stefan was eventually promoted again to his current rank. He'd had an opportunity to transfer to Air Station Miami but chose to remain in Clearwater. He'd fallen in love with the Gulf Coast and the Tampa area and had also made many friends there, in and out of the Coast Guard. Relocating and starting over hadn't even been an option for him when he'd been presented with the choice, and he'd turned down the transfer after only thinking it over for all of fifteen minutes—fourteen minutes longer than he'd truly needed.

Taking a deep breath, Stefan exhaled slowly. "Okay, sir, all bullshit aside. I no longer feel like a ninety-pound weakling that has to stand there and take it if a two-hundred-pound bully kicks sand in my face. That being said, I'm still not able to go toe to toe with one yet, either. I'd probably end up on my ass after half a round." It was the first time he'd admitted that to anyone, but his captain had earned and deserved the truth.

Stefan thought about Cassie—she deserved the truth too, especially since he didn't think she believed him whenever he told her he was just fine. She'd been over to his townhouse several times since the night she'd brought him dinner and caught him playing basketball. Word had spread among the neighborhood kids about Cassie's directive, and they were taking it seriously. Anytime Stefan was outside, while they were shooting hoops or playing catch or stickball, he could watch, but if he tried to join in, they'd say he wasn't allowed to.

At first, it'd annoyed him, but now it was a running joke. He would fake attempting to play, and there was always a chorus of "bugger off" when he did. It sounded like a bunch of Brits had invaded the neighborhood.

The first time Cassie had come over after that, Stefan had kinda suckered her in. He wasn't sure why he'd done it but was glad he had. He'd met with Vivian Dickson, the nutritionist, before his rehab session and had received a list of cardiac-friendly and -unfriendly foods. Surprisingly, prior to the heart attack, there had been some foods on his mostly healthy diet that he now had to eliminate and others he had to add. Using that, he'd played a little dumb and asked Cassie if she wouldn't mind helping him with the grocery shopping and cleaning out his pantry and refrigerator that following Friday, knowing she had no classes after work. He wasn't sure if she'd figured out it was just a ploy so he could spend time with her, but she'd agreed.

Since then, she'd come over often to help him try out several new heart-healthy recipes. He'd told her to bring her homework and study at his place if needed. While she did that, he cooked or caught up on his fiction reading. Stefan was enjoying those nights more than he'd expected to, and he missed his little pixie the nights she had class or other plans. So far, their time together had been strictly platonic, and while he would love to sink his cock into her sweet body again, he'd grown comfortable with their non-sexual time. In fact, he was craving it almost as much as their playtime when she wasn't there.

"How's the rehab going?" the captain asked.

He shrugged. "It's going. I keep trying to push myself, and the therapists and my body keep telling me not to."

He'd had his latest session that morning, and although it was nowhere near what he'd been doing before his heart attack, Dewayne had increased some of the weights and aerobic exercises. Cassie had given Stefan an encouraging smile when the therapist had rattled off the new speed and incline on his treadmill.

"You'll get there."

When the other man absentmindedly tapped his desk and didn't say anything more, Stefan stared at him, his damaged heart sinking. "Yeah, I'll get there . . . but not here, right?"

Lowe shook his head in obvious regret that he was the bearer of bad news. "I'm sorry, but no. I spoke to Commander Harrison this morning. He's recommending the MEB give you a medical discharge."

Stefan's entire body sagged. That last thread of hope had snapped in two. "Shit." He ran a hand down his freshly shaven face and thought for a few seconds. "I-I can appeal the decision, right?"

After a moment of silence, Lowe leaned forward and crossed his arms on his desk. "Yes, you can. It'll take a while for them to process everything, so you have a few weeks to decide to appeal if you think your cardiologist and therapists can convince the board you're fit for duty. But honestly, son, I think it'll be a waste of time. And even if you do somehow manage to have the decision overturned—which, after my conversation with Harrison, I doubt you'll be able to—you'll be looking at a desk job. Working in the SSC will no longer be an option. The Guard won't risk a commander, with a pre-existing heart attack that resulted in a cardiac arrest, having another life-threatening medical event in the middle of a critical rescue."

Fuck, he hadn't thought of that. A pencil-pushing desk job would suck more than sitting at home, twiddling his thumbs.

"Look, Stefan, this sucks—I get that—you're being forced out fifteen, twenty years before you were planning on leaving on your own terms. But things could've been a lot worse. First off, you're alive and will still be able to do most of the things you could do before, even if you're not one hundred percent yet. You're retiring at a rank with a good disability pension rate, on top of that trust fund you told me about, so buy yourself a boat, go fishing to your heart's content, find a good woman to settle down with, and see the world. I know some people don't realize it, but there's more to life than just the Guard. It's your turn to discover that."

Stefan let out a soft huff. Captain Lowe meant well since he'd been happily married to his wife of twenty-eight years, Cynthia. She was a marine biologist, and according to her husband, it'd been love at first sight. The captain was also on the tail end of his career, facing mandatory retirement in three years at the age of sixty-two. While some lifers didn't look forward to retirement, thinking they'd be bored out of their skull—Stefan now knew how they felt—Lowe was the complete opposite. He and Cynthia were already mapping out their road trip across the country in the RV they would purchase. Apparently, there was something called the Great American Bucket List—fifty things to do in the United States before you die. The Lowes planned to experience every one of them.

Stefan wondered if that was something Cassie would like to do someday . . . with him. He scrubbed the thought from his mind. He had other things he needed to think about than an unrealistic fantasy. Cassie had her whole life ahead of her with a new career and no health issues. She wouldn't want to be with a Dom who could drop dead before he was forty.

"Guess I don't have much choice. Have you told my command yet?"

"No. Thought you'd want to do that when you're ready."

He didn't think he'd ever be ready, but he appreciated Lowe leaving it up to him to tell his staff in the Incident Management Division. "Thank you, sir. I'll need a few days to wrap my head around this. I'll let you know when I make the announcement."

Picking up the box of San Lotano Requiem Maduro Toro cigars he'd brought in with him, Stefan got to his feet and handed it to Lowe. "It's been an honor and a privilege to serve under your command, Captain. Since cigars are on my list of things I'm no longer allowed to enjoy, I thought you'd like to have these. Sorry, but there's two missing—had them before the heart attack."

Lowe grinned and accepted the box before standing. "I have to admit, your medical issues have me rethinking some of my own habits, but these are too good to pass up. Thank you, Commander. It's also been *my* honor and a privilege to have *you* under my command all these years."

Stefan snapped to attention and saluted. "Thank you, sir."

The captain returned the salute. "Dismissed, Lieutenant Commander."

# Seventeen

Cass searched for the ringing cell phone in her purse as she walked from the parking lot, across the quad, to the building her Intro to Biology class was in at the Griffin College of Nursing in St. Petersburg. It was typically a forty-minute drive from her apartment near Tampa General Hospital to the school. Thankfully, her 7:00-3:00 p.m. shift in the rehab unit gave her enough time to go home, shower, eat, and relax for a little bit before she had to leave again for her six o'clock class. This evening, however, traffic had been on her side, and she'd arrived five minutes earlier than usual.

Finding the phone, she pulled it out and answered when she saw it was her younger sister calling from New Jersey. "Hey, Chris."

"Hey, Cass. Did I . . . um . . . did I call at a bad time?"

Cass stopped her forward momentum, closed her eyes, and inwardly sighed. Whenever Christine started a conversation off like that and sounded as if she'd been crying, it was never good. "Um, I have a few minutes, but I'm walking into class soon. What's wrong?" She bit back the urge to add, "This time."

There was a long pause, and for a moment, Cass thought they'd been disconnected before Christine spoke. "I left him for good, Cass."

Opening her eyes, she glanced around and saw an unoccupied bench nearby. Striding over, she took a seat and exhaled heavily. "What happened this time?" She hadn't been able to stifle the urge again.

Cass already knew the answer to the somewhat rhetorical question. Chris's husband of seven years was a lying, cheating bastard who couldn't keep it in his pants. They'd eloped right out of high school, despite both families' objections, and Randy had begun cheating on her about two months after the ink was dry on their marriage certificate. For some stupid reason, Christine kept taking him back. Thankfully, no children were involved—she'd been smart enough to stay on her birth control.

"Don't say it like that. I mean it this time. I packed up everything I own and moved in with Maureen." Well, that was something new. Usually, Chris went to their mother's when she was "leaving" Randy, but only took a suitcase full of stuff and said she'd go back for the rest later. Bringing everything she had and moving in with her best friend since second grade was something she'd never done before. "I'm done with him. He got some eighteen-year-old skank pregnant."

"Seriously?" Cass's eyes widened as she checked her watch. She had a few minutes before she had to be inside. "How'd you find out?"

"She knocked on my door the other day and told me."

"And you believed her? Just like that? Don't get me wrong—I wouldn't put it past Randy to be so careless and stupid."

The sound of a door shutting came over the phone. "At first, I didn't believe her. I just thought it was another one of his affairs, thinking he'd leave me for her. But she showed me the ultrasound, and when I said that it could be anyone's, she told me to call her gynecologist while she stood there. When I did, she gave the nurse who answered permission to confirm the pregnancy. The skank wants me to divorce him so she can marry him. I told her he's all hers. Mom's lawyer friend, Julie, started the divorce process for me this morning." Chris started sobbing. "I-I don't know wh-why I stayed with him, Cass. Wh-why didn't I listen to you and Mom?"

Cass's heart broke for her sister. "Because you loved him and thought he'd change for you. I'm sorry he didn't, but you're doing the right thing. You deserve to be happy and find someone who treats you like a queen."

So did Cass. These last few weeks, she and Stefan had grown closer than they'd ever been before, and yet their relationship had become totally platonic. She wasn't sure why he kept inviting her over, but she found she couldn't turn him down. Maybe she was a glutton for punishment, but she tried to convince herself she went there to help him get better, but that wasn't true—she kept going because she'd missed him too.

There had been no sex, play, or anything else between them—not even a kiss on the cheek. Instead, there had been heated stares from him when he thought she didn't see them and utter longing on her part for what they had now to be combined with what they'd had before. When she'd gone to his townhouse for dinner several times and hadn't been studying or watching a movie with him, they talked—really talked for the first time since they'd met.

He'd told her about his grandfather, who'd taught him how to tie nautical knots, which had led to Stefan's love of Shibari. They'd exchanged what their favorite things were—food, colors, etc.—and discussed current events, their own pasts, and the futures they dreamed of. Cass, of course, had held back some of those dreams from him, considering he starred in many of them.

"I know," her sister replied. "And someday, down the road, I'll start dating again. For now, though, I don't want to even look at another man." She huffed out a breath. "Anyway, enough about me. How's that guy you've been seeing? Stefan, right? Are you still together?"

"Listen, Chris," she said when she noticed a few classmates hurrying toward the entrance to the building. She was glad to have an excuse to avoid responding to the question she had no answer to, realizing she hadn't told her mom and sister she'd broken up with Stefan. Since they rarely came to Florida, had never met him, and were constantly asking if she was seeing someone, Cass had lied a little and told them she and Stefan had been dating. It'd also been wishful thinking at the time. "I have to get to class, but I'll call you later. Maybe you could come down here for a visit, you know, to get a change of scenery."

"I'd love that, Cass. Thank you." She sniffled. "I love you, sis."

"Love you two, sweetie. Tell Mom I'll call her tomorrow."

"I will. Bye."

"Bye."

Cass disconnected the call and rushed to class, only to find out the instructor hadn't arrived yet. Seeing her usual seat available next to Alyssa Hawthorne, Cass grabbed it and set her books down. "Hey, girl. What's up?"

The nineteen-year-old smiled at Cass. "Not much. I had an early dinner with Jake and Nick before coming here. I swear those two are so cute together, and that's not a word I ever thought I'd use for Jake."

She snorted as she organized her purse, phone, water bottle, pens, textbooks, and notebook. Alyssa was so sweet. While she'd heard some ugly rumors about how horrible the young woman's father had been, she wasn't sure how much of it was true, so she chose to believe only what Alyssa had told her one night over coffee after class.

Three years ago, Jake Donovan had helped Alyssa and her mom get away from a physically abusive father/husband—Cass didn't know the extent of the abuse—arranging for them to get new names and live somewhere else. Unfortunately, a year later, the bastard had somehow found them again and paid someone to kill them. Alyssa had managed to escape and contact Jake to help her. He'd brought her to a safe house somewhere. Then, he and Nick, his husband/submissive and brother to Ian and Devon, had rescued Alyssa when her father had tried a second time to kill her, and Nick had been shot in the process.

Thankfully, he'd recovered, and Alyssa's father had been killed instead. Since the young woman had no family left, the parents of Ben "Boomer" Michaelson had stepped in, offered to be her guardians, and recently moved with her to St. Petersburg. Ben was another operative at Trident and a Dom at the club. Cass had played with him many times before his high-school sweetheart, Kat, had come back into his life, and they'd fallen in love again and gotten married. Ben now considered Alyssa his sister, a fact she loved. She was also very close to Jake and Nick and saw them often. They'd been there for her every step of the way after all that nastiness had gone down.

Recently, Jake had helped her petition the courts to change her surname from Wagner to Hawthorne, her mother's maiden name, when she'd turned eighteen since the former had been her father's name, and she'd refused to keep it.

"What did they do that was cute? And you're right—cute is not a word for Jake. Nick? Yes. Jake? No." While both men were incredibly handsome, Jake was the broodier and quieter one and nine years Nick's senior. Nick was the vibrant, funny one who'd brought some much-needed light into his husband's life.

"Did you know they're talking about either adopting or using a surrogate?"

Cass grinned and lowered her voice as their instructor walked in the door. "I know. I'm so happy for them—they'll make great fathers."

A vision of a little boy with Stefan's soft, brown eyes floated into her mind. She could imagine Stefan teaching his son how to tie knots just like his grandfather had taught him. Her heart ached that she wouldn't be the one to give him a child. Yes, he wanted her—she knew that—but only in a Dominant, sexual way. What would she do if Stefan met someone who could change his mind about long-term relationships? Someone who he'd sign an open-ended contract with? It would kill her to see him with someone else.

She'd been right when she'd said her safeword and ended their monthly renewable contracts. And all she was doing now was setting herself up for more heartache. She'd been using the excuse of helping him recover from his heart attack as the reason she'd been seeing him so much, but he really didn't need her.

He'd made the lifestyle changes the nutritionist and cardiologist had suggested. He was eating healthy, getting stronger in rehab, taking his medications, getting rid of his cigars completely, and cutting down on his scotch. Stefan didn't need her for any of that—all he wanted was to top her and play with her—and it was best she withdrew from his life again before she lost her heart to him once more. But Cass feared it was already too late for that because she'd never gotten it back from the last time.

"How's the lieutenant commander doing?" Alyssa asked while the instructor spoke to one of the students in private. She'd met Stefan a few times at parties at the TS compound.

While she'd discovered a BDSM club there, she was still in the dark about who actually belonged to it. She knew the Trident owners, most of their employees, and their significant others were members since they were part of her extended family now. However, she wasn't privy to who else was unless they'd told her or spoken about the club in front of her. Cassie had admitted she was a member as she'd gotten to know Alyssa and the younger woman had figured out Stefan was one as well, but she didn't know the two had been in a D/s relationship for ten months.

"He's doing well." As far as Cass knew, that is. He was supposed to have met with his captain this morning, but she didn't know how it had turned out. She knew Stefan hadn't been looking forward to it, and he'd been kinda quiet last night during dinner. Cass had texted him that morning, wishing him luck, and then again, a few hours later, asking how the meeting had gone, but he hadn't responded to either.

"You know, you two would make a cute couple."

Before she could respond, the instructor announced the start of class. Thank God. She didn't want to think about her and Stefan as a couple—couldn't think it—because there was not a chance in hell of that happening.

# Eighteen

Pulling into Stefan's complex, Cass couldn't stop worrying about him. He hadn't been at rehab since last Friday, and today was the second session he'd missed. Oh, he'd called and told the cardiology department's secretary that he was just feeling a little under the weather and he'd be back soon, but Cass was finally calling bullshit. He hadn't answered the voicemails she'd left, checking up on him, and her texts had always been met with short, curt responses, such as, "I'm fine. Can't talk right now."

She'd waited impatiently for more dinner invites, but those hadn't been offered. Ever since his meeting with his captain, Stefan had shut down, and it was time for Cass to find out what was going on. She might not be his sub or his lover anymore, but damn it, she was his friend, and friends stood by each other through thick and thin. Whether Stefan liked it or not, she was butting her nose into his business.

Climbing out of her parked car, she waved at the four boys playing basketball two driveways down. They grinned and waved back.

"Hey, Cassie!"

"What's up, Cass?"

"Hi, Cassie!"

"Looking good, Cassie!"

Uh-huh. That last comment had come from Kenny Cooper—she bet he was popular with the girls at his school, the flirt. He was probably a man-whore in the making, but she doubted that would stop the ladies from falling at his feet.

Instead of going straight to Stefan's townhouse, she detoured toward the boys. "Hi, guys. Have any of you seen Stefan the last few days?"

They all looked at each other and then back at her. Marty Briggs was the one who shrugged and spoke up. "Not since last week. If we did, we would've told him to bugger off if he tried to join a game." The last was said with a grin.

Cass laughed for the first time since she'd left work on her way here. "And I thank you for that. I'll let you know when he's allowed to play again."

After saying goodbye, she strode up the walkway leading to Stefan's townhouse and knocked on his door. When there was no answer, she pounded harder. "Stefan, I know you're in there. Your truck's here. Open up because I'm not going away until you do." God, she sounded like a stalker or a bitchy ex-girlfriend. Hopefully, his neighbors didn't think that, too, and called the cops. "Stefan! Please? I'm worried."

The door swung open, and Cass couldn't believe her eyes. Stefan looked like shit. His eyes were bloodshot, he was unshaven with far more than a five o'clock shadow, and his clothes looked like he'd been in them for a few days. He swayed, and Cass lunged forward to grab him. Holy shit, he reeked of stale beer and sweat.

Her eyes narrowed as she steadied him. "Stefan, are you drunk?"

"Yup, I sure am. Come on in for a drink, babe."

*Babe?* He'd never called her that before, and she didn't like how degrading it sounded coming from his mouth. She preferred when he called her his little pixie. "Um . . . I'll come in, but I'll pass on the drink."

"Sssssuit yoursssself," he slurred.

When she cleared the threshold, he closed the door and then staggered into the living room, where he picked up a beer bottle and took a long swig. His place was a mess—beer bottles, half-filled plates, newspapers, unopened mail, and bags and containers from fast-food places were everywhere. This was not the man she knew. The real Stefan was a bit of a neat freak, probably due to his time in the Coast Guard.

"What're ya doin' here?" He eyed her salaciously. "Wanna play?"

Oh, boy, he was so freaking drunk if he'd asked her that question without reservation. In the past, if they were going to play, Master Stefan never had more than a sip or two of wine during dinner and never drank at the club before a scene. Even though there was a two-drink allowance at The Covenant before play, he'd always taken his role as a Shibari Master seriously and stayed sober until aftercare had been properly administered.

"I don't think that's a good idea, S—" The title Sir almost slipped out, but then she'd thought better of it. He wasn't acting like a responsible Dom at the moment and, therefore, didn't deserve the respect of one. "Why haven't you been to rehab since last week? You need it to help you recover."

"What for?" he spat out while glaring at her. "My career's over. What'd am I supposed to do now? Twiddle my fucking thumbs?" Again, he swayed but clumsily grabbed hold of the fireplace mantel before she could intervene. "Life sucks, so why bother with rehab?"

Rage roiled through her. Was he saying that if he couldn't be a Coastie, there was no point in living?

Balling her fists, she stepped forward into his personal

space, ignoring the height difference between them. Right now, she felt she was towering over him, even though the opposite was true. "How dare you! Do you realize how many people never get a do-over in life? You did! You were brought back from the dead for a second chance, and you're throwing it away like it doesn't matter. So, your carefully structured life isn't going the way you planned. Well, get over it, Stefan."

When he growled at her, she shook her finger in his face, not letting him get a word in edgewise. "Don't even think of pulling that Dom attitude on me. You're not acting like a Dom right now, and I'll be damned if I'll stand here and call you Sir or Master. I may be a sexual submissive, but that doesn't make me a doormat. You have people who care about you—*I* care about you. So do your parents, your sister, and all your friends and coworkers.

"Do you know how many people rushed to the hospital or kept calling for updates while you were in surgery? A fucking lot, I'll tell you that! People made sure your folks were taken care of. They sent food over. They offered to help out in any way they could. They *fucking prayed* for you because they didn't want to lose you—you're *that* important to them. And now, you're drinking, not coming to rehab, and doing God knows what else to put yourself back in the hospital or an early fucking grave." She stomped her foot. "How dare you! Well, you know what? I won't stand here and watch you throw your life down the drain, Stefan. Do you know why? Because it hurts too damn much."

She spun on her heel and stalked across the room before pivoting back toward him. "You know, I'm glad I didn't renew our contract. You're not the man I thought you were. The Stefan I knew loved life—he lived it to the fullest. I'm not sure I even want to know this side of you. In fact, I know I don't. Goodbye, Stefan."

Cass didn't bother waiting for a response from him. For

the second time in as many months, she fled his townhouse, holding back the tears until she reached her car. Once she was in the driver's seat, they burst forth. Glancing up, she saw Stefan standing in the open doorway of his unit, staring at her, and she hoped he couldn't see her crying. He stayed there as she started the engine, put the gear in drive, and pulled out of the parking lot.

Needing someone to talk to, instead of going home alone, Cass steered the car toward the Trident Security compound. Before she'd arrived at Stefan's, Sasha had sent her a text saying she was visiting with Angie and Kristen and invited her to join them. The women would be there for her like she'd been there for them whenever they needed her. And she needed them more than ever right now.

———

"He said what?" Angie demanded as she continued to breastfeed her daughter. Kristen's son, JD, was sitting on the floor next to Sasha, making something with plastic blocks. The cottage was on the west side of the fenced-in property and had been built as a shared studio for Kristen, an author, and Angie, an artist, after finding they ended up in either one's apartment almost every day. The cottage had plenty of windows to give Angie natural light to work with. Each woman had her own space, and there was a play area, a kitchenette, and a full bath available.

Cass just nodded as Kristen handed her a cup of tea. Angie's question had obviously been rhetorical, so she didn't bother repeating what Stefan had said.

Handing JD another block, Sasha asked, "What did you say to him?"

She gave them the abridged version of how she'd berated Stefan, and the women hooted.

"Good for you," Angie cheered.

"Men." Sasha rolled her eyes. "How can they be Doms and such stupid idiots at the same time?" Probably out of habit, she glanced over her shoulder and then around the room. "Just checking there are no Doms around."

Before anyone could say anything else, the cottage's front door swung open, and Ian strode in. Sasha's brown skin paled, and she froze. The other women cast worried looks at each other. As Ian approached the group, it became obvious he hadn't heard the submissive calling Doms "stupid idiots," and they all relaxed again. When he heard the entire story, he would probably agree with them, but it was still disrespectful to call Doms names.

"Hello, ladies." The man smiled as he bent over and kissed Angie's lips before doing the same to Peyton's forehead. The little girl's face lit up at the sight of her father, and she let go of her mother's nipple. Taking the cloth his wife had placed over her shoulder for when she burped the baby, Ian threw it over his own shoulder and then reached down to take his daughter. He was a handsome man, any day of the week, but put a baby in his arms, and he was beyond McDreamy.

"Came over to get your baby fix?" Angie teased as she adjusted her shirt and nursing bra.

"Yup, and to give us both a break. I've got a boring conference call in ten minutes that'll probably go on well over an hour, so I figured my sweet little girl could keep me company for a bit, and we could have some bonding time. That gives you a chance to do whatever you need to do."

Cass's heart melted, and by the looks on the other women's faces, theirs had too. Apparently, Ian had installed a crib, a changing table, and a few other baby items in a corner of his office over in the Trident Security building, so his daughter could visit with him any time he wanted. Kristen had mentioned Devon had a similar arrangement in his office as well. The compound they were all in was a great setup for the Sawyer family. All Kristen, Devon, Ian, Angie, Nick, and Jake had to do was walk from the building that housed their penthouse-sized apartments to their respective work buildings. They could go back and forth whenever they needed or wanted to.

The same went for the club. Just had to walk across the compound, and *boom*, they were at The Covenant. Cass wasn't sure what would happen when the kids got old enough to realize there was a sex club less than a football field's distance from their homes, but the adults had plenty of time to figure that all out.

"Cassandra, what's wrong?"

She lifted her chin to find Ian studying her face, which was still red and puffy from crying all the way from Stefan's to there. His intense gaze showed he was truly concerned about her, which made her eyes well up again.

Angie reached over, patted her hand, and answered for her. "She went to check on Stefan because he'd missed some rehab sessions, and apparently, he's having a temper tantrum over the fact he's being forced to retire from the Coast Guard."

"Temper tantrum?"

Cass nodded and wrung her hands together. "I guess you could call it that. He was drunk and looked like he had been for a few days. The townhouse was a mess, and he wasn't acting like the Stefan we all know. I'm . . . really worried."

Ian's eyes narrowed at her as he rubbed Peyton's back, trying to elicit a burp from the infant. "What do you mean?"

"I don't think he's showered or changed his clothes in days, and there were beer bottles, used plates and bowls, newspapers, and a bunch of fast food bags all over the place. I don't even know if he's taking his medication." Her tears began to fall again. "When I asked him why he hadn't been to rehab, he basically said why he should bother going because his career and life were over."

She took the tissue Kristen handed her and wiped her eyes. "He could barely stand up without holding onto something and even asked if I wanted to . . . to play."

A low growl from Ian was interrupted by a loud belch from Peyton. Anger flared in his eyes, and his jaw clenched, but his gentle hold on the baby didn't change. The Covenant's head Dom took his position and participation in the BDSM lifestyle seriously, and he instantly fell into the role. "You didn't play with him while he was drunk, did you, subbie?"

Cass shook her head. "No, Sir, I refused."

"She told him off," Sasha announced. "Big time."

Ian's facial expression relaxed a bit. "Good." Cass figured that one word was in response to her not playing with the drunken Stefan and not the fact she'd told him off. "All right. Cassandra, for now, I want you to stay away from him. He's obviously not in a good place, mentally, and I don't want to see you hurt. I'll talk to him tomorrow and get his head out of his . . ." He glanced down at Peyton and then JD. "Out of his butt. Until then, I don't want you going to see him, understood?"

When she nodded, he added, "That goes for the rest of you too, ladies. No interfering."

"Yes, Sir," the submissives said in unison.

# Nineteen

"God damn it. I swear, the people in my life are fucking idiots sometimes. I'm getting sick of it," Ian bitched as he pulled into Stefan's townhouse complex at just after eight in the morning.

Beside him, Mitch snorted. "Right. Because you've never been a fucking idiot in your entire life. Get real, cuz."

"I've been an idiot before, but not a *fucking* idiot. *Fucking* idiots are worse than regular idiots, and I've only been a regular idiot a few times."

Mitch looked at him incredulously. "What's the difference?"

After pulling into a spot, he put the gearshift into Park. "The difference is an idiot doesn't realize he's screwing up until someone points it out to him. A *fucking* idiot knows he's screwing up and doesn't do a damn thing about it, even when the best thing he's ever had is staring at him in the face."

Ian hadn't been too surprised when he'd learned from Cassandra that Stefan was in a depressive funk and acting like a putz about his Coastie career being over. Shit happened. The guy had to get over it. Besides, working in the private sector was a lot more fun and financially secure—not that Ian nor Stefan needed the money.

Getting out of the truck, he met Mitch at the tailgate before striding toward Stefan's unit. Mitch gave him a sideways glance and a grin. "Have you consulted your 'twat roster' and decided on a new nickname for him yet?"

"Yup."

A few seconds passed before Mitch prodded, "Well?"

When Ian still didn't respond, the other man stopped short. "What? You're not going to tell me whatever nickname you're going to be calling him in what? Thirty seconds?"

Smirking, he kept walking. "Nope. Life's a bitch, ain't it?"

*Less than* thirty seconds later, he knocked loudly on Stefan's door. "Hey, twat-knot, open the damn door!"

Mitch chuckled as he stepped up next to him. "Love it."

After another round of pounding on the door, it finally swung open, and Ian eyed the man on the other side of the threshold. "Damn, you look like crap. I thought, after a few weeks, you were supposed to look better than when you were actually having your heart attack."

Stefan frowned and scowled at them with bloodshot eyes. His clothes were disheveled, and he probably hadn't changed them in days. He also hadn't shaved at any time within the past week or so. "Whatta you doin' here?"

"Don't you know an intervention when you see one, twat-knot? Okay, so it's only the two of us, but truthfully, all you really need is me kicking your ass to get it back in line." He pushed the door open further, forcing Stefan back a step, and strolled inside. "Mind if we come in? Not that I care whether you do or not, but I thought I'd try being polite for a change."

He inspected the place as he strolled through it. Cassandra had accurately described it to him yesterday. The kitchen was a mess with empty pizza, Mexican, Chinese, and fast food containers and bags, and beer bottles. "Since when do you eat fast food?" He hitched a thumb toward the kitchen as he moved into the living room. "I'm pretty sure none of that shit's on your nutritionist's checklist."

His gaze roamed the space. Used plates, more empty beer bottles, and several newspapers were strewn about the seating area. Ian glanced at one of the papers left open on the coffee table. "Seriously? You're looking for a job in the local want ads? Doing what? Cleaning out toilets or frying hamburgers? Selling used cars? Serving popcorn to little shits at the movie theater? There's nothing wrong with those jobs if that's all you can get or those are the only ones you're qualified to do. But last time I checked, your intelligence and skill set make you overqualified for any of those jobs. Although, I *am* starting to question your intelligence."

During Ian's rambling, Mitch had shaken his head and then disappeared into the kitchen before returning with a box of garbage bags. He quietly set about cleaning up the living room as Stefan plopped down in his recliner and glared at him. The homeowner still hadn't said a single word to his uninvited guests aside from his surly greeting.

After a few moments of silence, Stefan turned his glare to Ian, who was leaning against the wall with his arms crossed. "I don't need or want a fucking intervention, Sawyer. I'm fine, and how I live my life is none of your damn business."

"Yeah, because you look fine." Ian snorted. "As for this being none of my business, you're wrong there too. This *is* my business—you're a Dom in my club, a friend, and fellow member of the military—although the Coasties are faux-military." Of course, he had to get that dig in. "And I won't sit back and watch you slowly kill yourself."

Leaning back, Stefan rolled his bloodshot eyes. "I'm not trying to kill myself, asshole."

His eyebrows shot up, and he gestured to the messy room that Mitch was taking care of. "No? Because it sure looks that way to me. You just had a major heart attack, you're eating junk food that probably hasn't passed through your colon since you were a teen, you're drinking to excess, and you've bailed on your rehab sessions. Ten to one, you haven't even been taking your new meds lately."

When Stefan wouldn't look at him, Ian knew his suspicion was correct. *Damn idiot.*

He was done with this shit. Reaching around to his lower back, he pulled out his concealed, holstered 9mm and set it on the side table next to the recliner. Mitch froze and stared at his cousin like he had three heads, but Ian ignored him. Instead, he pointed at the gun and addressed Stefan. "You want to kill yourself, go right ahead. But why fucking drag it out? That's fully loaded, and one's in the chamber. Just pick it up, point it at your head, and pull the goddamn trigger. Fast and easy, and the rest of us don't have to sit back and watch you kill yourself over the next few months." He shrugged. "So, just do it now, and we'll give you a proper funeral, then get on with our lives."

Stefan ran a hand down his whiskered face and released a low growl. "You're a fucking bastard, you know that?"

"Not according to my parents—they were happily married before they were blessed with my conception."

After a few moments of tense silence, Stefan picked up the gun and handed it back to Ian, who clipped it to the waistband of his pants at his lower back again. "Good choice, twatknot."

"God, don't tell me that's my new nickname."

Ian grinned. "Yup, it is. I've already penciled it in on my twat roster. I love that freaking thing—everybody should have one." Sitting next to Mitch on the now cleared sofa, he set his ankle on the opposite knee. "Now that we've gotten your impending suicide out of the way, let's talk about other shit. So, your time in the Guard is up, huh?"

"How did you . . ." Stefan's eyes narrowed. "Let me guess—Cassie told you."

"She's worried about you—God knows why. What I don't get, Commander, is why you've got your panties in a twist—it's not like you need the fucking money."

Sighing, Stefan picked up a half-full beer bottle, stared at it a moment, then put it back on the side table. He stood up and paced back and forth in front of them. "It's not about the damn money, and you know it. It's about doing a job I love. It's about saving lives and being part of something that *means* something. I didn't plan on retiring for another twenty, twenty-five years." He stopped and stared at them as if he were hoping they'd give him words of wisdom. "Now, what am I supposed to do?"

"Start a new chapter in your life," Mitch said, speaking for the first time.

"Exactly," Ian agreed. "Look, what I'm about to say is not out of fucking pity or anything, so don't take it that way. I was talking to Dev and the rest of Trident's new co-owners—God, what was I thinking when I gave the Alpha Team shares of the company? Anyway, we talked about it and agreed we want you to come work for us."

Stefan gaped as he sat in the recliner again. "What? Are you kidding me?"

Shaking his head, Ian held up a hand, staving off any objection until the other man heard him out. "Not as an operative—at least not until you get cleared by the doctors as being one-hundred percent again—but as a trainer. We've bought up some more land to the west of the compound, and we're starting a new venture.

"We'll be running training classes for law enforcement and private security, teaching them tricks of the trade the military and black ops use that the locals haven't had the opportunity to learn. Some sessions will be only a day or two, while others might be longer, covering hostage rescue, active shooter situations, OCONUS details, corporate bodyguards, et cetera, and whatever else you can think of that will interest our clients. We'll also offer a chance for SWAT teams to come in for practice runs, evaluations, and modification training. While larger police departments have their own facilities and instructors, smaller departments don't always have that luxury, so sometimes their training isn't up to par.

"We sent out query letters to numerous departments in Florida to see if there was a need for this kind of setup, and the response has been very positive. Several departments want to be in on the first classes. We're certain once we get started, we'll have interest up and down the East Coast.

"So, we need someone to run the whole shebang. You'd oversee scheduling both the sessions and instructors. You'll have opportunities to teach as well. On top of that, you'll also take over training and firearms qualifications for all Trident team members and our Personal Protection Division, except for the K9 training—Kat Michaelson will still be in charge of that. Trust me, you'll have plenty of things to do to keep you busy, and the pay and benefits will be a lot better than you had in the Guard too."

When Stefan just sat there, slack-jawed, staring at him, Ian continued. "As I mentioned, this isn't a pity thing, man. We need someone highly qualified, who can teach and develop different training ideas. Marco was in charge of firearms qualifications, but with his family now and Harper being pregnant again—"

Stefan's eyebrows lifted. "Seriously? Wow, good for him."

"Yeah, I don't think he's stopped grinning since he found out. You'd never know he'd been allergic to marriage and kids a while back. Anyway, what do you say? Are you in, or are you going to order another round of fast food and proceed to trash your house again?"

A snort was his response. "You're really an ass, you know that?"

"So I've been told numerous times. Tick-tock, Lundquist. What's it gonna be?"

He shook his head, then winced and stopped as if the act had caused him some agony. From the number of empty beer bottles Mitch had thrown out, it probably had. "I don't know. Hell, if the Coast Guard doesn't want me, then . . . seriously, Ian, a desk job with you would be just as bad as a desk job with the Guard."

Tilting his head back, Ian spoke to the ceiling. "Why am I surrounded by twatwaffles? I mean, what have I ever done to piss you off so much that these people give me grief? Huh?"

He returned his attention to Stefan. "It's not a fucking desk job. Will you be sitting at a desk some of the time, filling out paperwork and typing shit into the computer? Yeah, absolutely. Even I have to do that. Will you be doing other shit outside the office? Fuck, yeah. Hell, if your doctor okays it, I'll even send you up in the helicopter with Babs for one of her roller coaster rides if you want. But I should warn you—bring a barf bag."

He leaned forward, placing his arms on his knees. "Look, twat-knot. This isn't a pity job offer, nor are you going to be twiddling your thumbs half the time. Once your cardiologist gives you the green light, I want your ass showing these guys how things are done when the shit hits the fan. I don't offer people jobs just because they're my friends. You've got the right stuff for this position, but if you don't want it, feel free to pass and apply for a job at McDonald's or Burger King. I'm sure they could use a guy with SAR training to make some fries."

Long seconds passed as the man thought it over. Ian knew he would say yes at some point—Stefan just needed to let the shock wear off before the offer settled in his hungover mind.

Ian had told him the truth, this wasn't a pity job offer. He knew the lieutenant commander had been a damn good Coastie and had the leadership skills to excel in the private sector.

Finally, Stefan nodded. "I want to see the program's business plan before I give a definite yes, but yeah, I think I'm in."

Ian grinned. "Glad to hear it. Since you're still on medical leave from the Guard, you can start next week if you'd like. There's a lot of setup that needs to happen before the first sessions can be announced. I'll email you the business plan, and if you've got any details or suggestions you'd like to add to it, let me know."

Stefan's gaze shot to Mitch. "Why'd you tag along?"

Ian's cousin shrugged. "Last time he held an intervention like this, he and Chase Dixon dumped buckets of ice water on their buddy, Tuff, while he was sleeping off a drunken stupor in bed. I came along to make sure he didn't do the same to you." He smirked. "You know, since you're recovering from a major heart attack and all."

A bark of laughter erupted from Stefan, and he smiled for the first time since they'd gotten there. "Thanks, I appreciate it."

"So, does this mean you're going to start your rehab and meds again and cut out all this other crap?"

He sighed. "Yeah, I'm a dumbass, and I'll get my act straight again."

"You're not a dumbass—you're a twat-knot." Ian got to his feet and gave the Shibari Master a black look that had made many men almost pee in their pants. He fisted his hands. "And if I ever . . . *ever* hear of you suggesting to a sub that you play while you're three sheets to the wind again, I'll kick your fucking ass—no-holds-barred. Got it?"

A queasy look came over the other man's face, and he winced. "Yeah, I know I fucked up and owe Cassie an apology.

I wouldn't have really gone through with it—I think I was hoping she'd leave because I didn't want to deal with her right then. Regardless, I swear it won't happen again."

"It better not." His hands relaxed again. "Now that that's all taken care of, come by the club later—you haven't been there in weeks, and we've got a big surprise happening tonight around eight."

"What's going on?" Stefan asked as he stood.

Rolling his eyes, Ian started for the front door. "It wouldn't be a surprise if I fucking told you, now would it?"

A few minutes later, Mitch and Ian were back in the truck, exiting the complex. Mitch eyed his cousin with both amusement and curiosity. "So, what's this big surprise at the club?"

"Hell if I know—I just wanted him to get his ass back there." And together with the woman who'd fallen in love with him. "I've got a few hours to think of something."

# Twenty

Pulling into the club parking lot, Stefan hit redial on his phone one more time. Once again, Cass's voicemail kicked in. *Damn it.*

He'd been calling her all day to apologize for being a horse's ass—yeah, he wasn't calling himself a twat-knot—to her yesterday, but she hadn't returned any of his calls or responded to his texts. Turnabout was fair play, apparently, since he hadn't accepted any of her calls all week, and his texts had been short and not so sweet. He'd been tempted several times to call Mitch and get her home address—yes, he was a dick for not knowing where she lived—so he could swing by to see her. But he wasn't sure if the club owner would give it to him. He also wasn't sure if Cassie would slam the door in his face. He wasn't ready for that humiliation yet.

Stefan should've admitted to himself there was a life outside of the Guard, but he'd been too caught up in losing out on the carefully laid plans he'd made for the rest of his career. His goal had been to retire at the rank of Captain or higher. But after Cassie and then Ian had reamed his ass, he'd realized there was so much more to life. There were family, friends, and adventures.

And then there was Cassie. She'd walked out of his life twice now. This second time was his fault, without a doubt, but he'd never gotten around to finding out why she'd said her safeword and declined to sign their last contract. The more he thought about it now, the *more* it bugged him. And the *more* it bugged him, the more he realized she meant more to him than any other sub ever had—*more* than any other woman ever had. A life without Cassie in it looked kind of bleak to him, whether he was in or out of the Guard, but he didn't know if he had a chance to get her back now. Especially not after he'd screwed up yesterday.

After Ian and Mitch had left that morning, Stefan had finished cleaning up the rest of his place, then showered, steaming the last of the alcohol out of his system, and shaved. While eating a breakfast of egg whites, spinach, mushrooms, and low-fat cheese, he read through the prospectus Ian had emailed him. Stefan was impressed with the plans and details, although he hadn't expected anything less. The Sawyer brothers had built a successful security business, with individual, corporate, and government clients and contracts, over the past six or seven years since leaving their careers with the Navy SEALs behind. They'd hired fellow SEALs, in addition to members of other military branches and law enforcement. From what Stefan knew from interacting with most of them, both in and out of the club, none had any regrets about leaving their respective careers to enter the private sector. If they could do it, so could Stefan.

From what he'd seen in the business plan, Ian had been right—there would be plenty to keep Stefan busy. With his medical issues, he might not ever be able to go out into the field, but since reaching the rank of Lieutenant Commander, he'd been directing the rescues from the Sector Command

Center anyway instead of participating in them. He'd also been sharing his years of experience in SARs with the next generation of team members, ensuring they were ready for anything that could go FUBAR. Now, he was being given the chance to help train operatives and police officers, so he would still be working with the next generation, just in the private sector.

*When one door closes, another one opens, right? Or was it a window that opened? Oh, who the hell cares?* All he knew was his professional life was back on track again, and he'd get his health back there too, but now he had to work on his private life. And that meant he had to figure out what he would do about Cassie.

Did he want more than a D/s relationship with her? Did she want more? And with him? Would she want to risk being with a man who'd already died once?

And what about him? Was he willing to risk offering her more than he'd ever given another woman only to find out she didn't want it? Did he miss her because he'd gotten comfortable with her or because she'd become special to him? He was afraid to even think of the word "love," but is that what he felt for her?

*God, it shouldn't be this hard to figure this shit out, right?*

"Argh! Fuck this!" He exited the truck and slammed the door a little harder than necessary. He didn't even know why he'd showed up at the club tonight. He couldn't give two flying fucks what the surprise was because Cassie wouldn't be there—it was Thursday, and she had a class tonight. Maybe there was a chance she'd stop by afterward, although he doubted it. Not after she'd worked all day, then rushed to school for three hours of class.

"Master Stefan, it's so good to see you. How're you feeling?" Charlotte Roth, a.k.a. Mistress China, asked as she strolled across the parking lot toward him, dressed in a black catsuit and red thigh-high boots, with Mike Donovan on her heels. Mike owned Donovan's Pub, but here, he was the gorgeous Mistress's submissive boyfriend. It'd been a bit of a culture shock for Mike when he'd been drawn into the lifestyle by Charlotte, but he seemed to be adjusting nicely for someone who was an alpha male outside the club and their bedroom.

"I'm doing well, Mistress. Thank you." He gave her a friendly peck on her cheek. "Hello, Mike."

The other man bowed his head in respect for a moment. Anywhere else, Mike would've offered his hand to shake, but at the club, he was a submissive, and Stefan was a Dom, whom he had to defer to with respect and proper protocol. "Hello, Sir. You're looking much better than when I saw you in the hospital."

"I feel much better. Not a hundred percent yet, but getting there. Thanks again for sending over all the food. That hospital crap wasn't edible most of the time." Mike had arranged for someone to bring Stefan a healthy and tasty lunch and dinner every day after he'd been moved from the CCU to the step-down unit.

"I was happy to do it. Cassie had given me a list of menu items that were your favorites so I could make them for you."

Stefan wasn't surprised to hear that. She'd been on top of everything that had to do with his recovery. It warmed him to know she'd gone through so much trouble to take care of him, then it chilled him when he remembered how much of a douche he'd been to her yesterday.

The trio started walking toward the staircase that would take them to the second story of the former warehouse that now housed The Covenant on the east side of the Trident Security compound.

"Any idea what surprise event is happening tonight?" Stefan asked.

Charlotte frowned and shook her head. "I didn't know there was a special event tonight. Do you know anything about it, Michael?"

"No, Mistress. I haven't heard anything about it either."

"Hmm. Well, then, let's go find out, shall we?"

Moments later, they entered The Covenant's lobby. Stefan was greeted by several Doms and submissives, welcoming him back and inquiring about his current state as Charlotte and Mike continued into the main portion of the club. Word had obviously spread throughout the club's membership, and for the first time, he found it didn't bother him that everyone knew about his heart attack—at least not there. The members of The Covenant tended to be one big family. They looked out for each other. They celebrated accomplishments and milestones and grieved losses with each other. And they occasionally fought and made up as most families did.

As he approached the big, double wooden doors that led to the main club, Travis "Tiny" Daultry grinned at him, his pearly whites bright in contrast to his dark skin, and held out his hand. The six-foot-eight mountain of a man was the head of security for both the club and the compound. "Stefan, my man. Good to see you back. Heard you might be joining the crew on the other side of the fence."

He was apparently referring to the chain-link fence that separated the club from the rest of the Trident Security compound.

Stefan shook the man's hand, which was almost the size of a baseball glove. "Hey, Tiny. It's good to be back. And I'm thinking about it. Haven't given the boys a definite yes yet, but I'm leaning toward it."

"Glad to hear it." He opened one of the doors for Stefan. "Have a good time tonight."

"Thanks." Stefan strode in, and the familiar sights, sounds, and smells of the sex club immediately assaulted his senses. As always, they soothed him in a way most vanilla people could never understand.

More people greeted him as he made his way to the bar to grab a bottle of water. The last thing he needed tonight was more alcohol. He'd finally gotten the remnants of yesterday's binge out of his system, and he didn't need another hangover tomorrow. He'd even gone so far as to dump the remaining six bottles of beer from the eighteen-pack he'd torn through yesterday. It was time to get back on his healthy diet again too.

After getting his drink and chatting with a few people at the bar, he strolled to the top of the grand staircase and gave his membership card to the bouncer standing there. The card was scanned for the number of alcoholic drinks Stefan had been served—which was zero—and then returned to him. There was a two-drink maximum before entry to the play areas was denied. The bouncer nodded, signaling Stefan was cleared to head down to the pit.

The place was hopping. Music pounded from the overhead speakers, but it still didn't drown out the screams of pain and ecstasy coming from the play areas below. The scents of leather, citrus, and sex co-mingled enticingly. Doms and subs in a varying array of fet-wear were either playing, observing scenes, or just enjoying some conversation with like- and open-minded people.

At the bottom of the staircase, Stefan found Mitch with his submissives, Tyler and Tori—he was engaged to both—chatting with Brody and Fancy Evans. Stefan greeted both Doms with a handshake, gave a nod hello to Tyler, who was a switch in submissive mode as indicated by the collar he wore, and then kissed both women on the cheek.

"It's good to see you, Fancy," Stefan said with a smile. He hadn't seen Brody's wife at the club since she'd given birth a little over four months ago. "How's little Zane doing? Is he over in the new child-care center?"

With more and more of the Trident Security teams and their close friends having kids, a new little cottage had been added to the compound on the other side of the parking lot from the club. Several submissives were scheduled to spend a few hours babysitting, and the time went toward their membership fees, just like the wait staff, front desk attendants, and the three women who alternated working in the boutique.

"He's doing great, Sir," the curvaceous, auburn-haired beauty responded. "He's growing like a weed, cute as a bug, and laughs all the time. He's definitely his father's son, I'll tell you that."

Brody grinned and puffed out his chest. "Damn right, he is."

Fancy giggled as her husband tucked her into his side. "But Zane's still too young to bring him to child care, so our next-door neighbors, Amy and Kevin, offered to watch him for a few hours so we could have a night out. Their twins, Taylor and McKenna, are madly in love with him. They can't wait until they're old enough to babysit him on their own."

Stefan had a vague memory of the six-year-old girls who lived next door to "Mista Brophy" and "Mrs. Fancy," as they so fondly called the couple. "So, what's this surprise Ian's talking about? No one seems to know anything about it."

"Actually," Mitch began, "Ian's waiting for you over at the center stage."

His eyes narrowed in confusion. "Me? What for?"

"He needs your help with something, twat-knot." The submissives did their best to hide amused grins as Mitch chuckled. "I really get a kick out of that one."

Groaning at the new nickname, Stefan crossed his arms and waited a moment, expecting the club's co-owner to fill in the blanks of the surprise a little more, but the man wasn't forthcoming. From Mitch's and Brody's grins, though, it was clear they were up to something, and whatever it was, Ian was probably the one who'd come up with the idea. And that made Stefan very nervous.

He wondered if it was too late to hightail it out of there, and Brody confirmed his fear. "Don't be a chickenshit and leave—it's nothing bad."

Well, at least one jackass wasn't calling him a twat-knot. Glancing around, Stefan huffed. "Fine, but I really hate surprises. He better remember that shocking someone who recently had a fucking heart attack isn't the brightest thing to do."

"Don't worry," Mitch said with a grin. "I made sure the defibrillators were all in working order earlier."

"Asshole," Stefan replied without any heat behind it. He'd rather deal with sarcasm and friendly banter than everyone's sympathy. "All right, let me get this over with."

Leaving the small group, he walked across the room, stopping several more times when people said, "Hello," and asked how he was feeling. When he reached the center stage, Ian stood there talking to T. Carter. Unlike most members, Stefan knew the physically fit, blond man was a government spy for a black-ops agency ninety-nine percent of US law enforcement and military personnel had never heard of. His submissive/girlfriend, Jordyn, was a fellow agent too. That much Stefan knew—what he didn't know was the agency's name and what the damn "T" stood for. Apparently, the Dom hated the name he'd been given at birth and had been known as T. or Carter since his teens.

"Dude!" Carter held out his hand and, when Stefan shook it, pulled him into a man-hug and slapped his back a few times. "Glad to see you upright and breathing. How're you feeling?"

"Better, but it'll be a little while longer before I'm back in full fighting condition." After a quick glance around, he asked, "Where's Jordyn?"

"Business trip," was the vague response. In other words, she was on a covert mission somewhere, and Carter couldn't discuss it.

Ian nudged the operative's shoulder. "Yeah, but at least you could show up—and not just for the food."

The other man barked out a laugh. "With Jordy missing, I'm not sampling anything *but* the food, my friend."

Stefan had no idea what the obvious inside joke was about, so he turned his attention back to Ian with a glare. "So, what's this damn surprise no one seems to know about, Boss-man?"

His shoulders went up and down in nonchalance. "Nothing big, I assure you. I just figured for a welcome back celebration for you, we'd have a Shibari contest."

"Huh?" He eyed the stage. The St. Andrew's Cross had been pushed back to the far end, and several small tables with ropes atop them were evenly spaced across the width of the raised platform. "I'm the only Shibari Master in the club—isn't it a bit unfair for me to compete against other Doms?"

While there were several Dominants with rope play experience at The Covenant, Stefan's years of training put him out of their leagues.

"Who said you'd be competing? You're the judge."

Okaaayyyy. That wasn't as bad of a "surprise" as he'd expected. In fact, although he hadn't known about it until now, it really wasn't a big deal, so he had no idea why Ian hadn't just told him about it earlier. "All right. It'll be kind of interesting to see what my pupils have learned. I assume the Doms will be ones I've trained and cleared, correct?"

"Of course."

Without another word, Ian climbed the few steps to the stage and picked up a microphone that'd been on the floor. While Stefan should've been at ease at the turn of events, he was still getting a strange vibe from the Dom-in-residence. Ian was up to something.

When the man tapped the microphone, someone lowered the music that filled the club. "I hope everyone's having a good time tonight, as usual. We have an unannounced event taking place tonight to welcome back Master Stefan. Give the sorry bastard a round of applause for returning from the dead."

The club thundered as members clapped, whistled, and shouted at Stefan as Ian indicated for him to step up onto the stage. Embarrassed, he joined the other Dom, then just nodded and mouthed his thanks to the crowd before waving his hands, gesturing for them to quiet down.

"We have five Doms competing tonight," Ian announced, "in a Shibari contest. Master Stefan will be the judge. The winner and their submissive will receive a free month of membership to the club." Considering what the monthly dues were, that was a nice prize.

Pulling a piece of paper from a small pocket in his leather vest, he continued. "Competitors, as I call out your name, please escort your submissive to the stage. You'll have five minutes to inspect your equipment and get your sub in the starting position you desire. Master Dimitri. Master Zach. Master Renzo. Mistress Camilla. And Master Cain.

One by one, the Dominants made their way to the stage, leading their submissives. Two of the subs—one male, one female—were wearing collars, signaling the fact they were in a contracted D/s relationship. But the other three didn't have any adornment on their necks. If a certain one of them had, Stefan would've killed Cain Foster, a member of Trident's Omega Team and a former Secret Service agent—not that the man's occupations mattered to Stefan. What *did* matter was Foster's sub was none other than Cassie.

Stefan's jaw and fists clenched as he watched Foster escort Cassie up the steps. Her gaze was on the floor in submission. Tonight, she was wearing one of Stefan's favorite corset sets—a red and black, lacy number with a thong, and it pissed him off even more, considering he'd given it to her as a birthday present a few months back.

Unable to take his eyes off Cassie as Foster pointed for her to kneel on the pillow next to the last table set up for the contest, Stefan let out a low growl in Ian's direction. "What the hell are you up to, Sawyer?"

An exaggerated expression of innocence appeared on the other man's face. "Up to? I don't know what you're talking about. The unattached Doms selected their own subs. This is just a simple Shibari competition—no sex involved. Well, that is, unless the Doms and subs agreed to it in their negotiations."

The thought of Cassie having sex with Foster, or any other man, had Stefan's blood boiling. She was his, damn it!

But she really wasn't. They had no contract between them, and he'd removed her collar at her request. All Stefan could do was concede that Cassie was a free sub who could scene with whomever she wanted. Now, he just had to figure out how to get through judging the event without killing one of the competitors.

# Twenty-One

*Yup, I'm a manipulative bastard—no offense to Mom and Dad, of course.*

Ian led Stefan over to a small table with three chairs in the left front corner of the stage as the Doms prepared to start their rope play. Mitch was already sitting there. If this thing played out as Ian hoped, he and his cousin would need to take over the judging of the contest when four couples remained.

*The Coastie is fit to be tied—excuse the pun. Nah, don't excuse it . . . it was intentional and pretty funny if you ask me.*

Chuckling quietly at his own joke, Ian sat between the two men and waited for the fireworks to begin. After filling Cain in on the scheme, the other Dom had been more than happy to participate. Mitch, Carter, and Devon were the only other people who knew what was going on—hell, Cassandra didn't even know. Ian had done that for a few reasons. He'd wanted her reactions to be real, and as a Dom, Ian could be sneaky and get away with it. After basically ordering Cassandra to be Cain's submissive for the competition, he'd given her the only out he doubted she would take—her safeword.

Ian had always had a soft spot for the pretty blonde. Of course, not in a brotherly way since he'd had his fingers in her pussy and ass at one time. And not in a romantic way, either. But he'd always hoped he could find the perfect Dom for her. Stefan was that Dom—Ian knew it deep in his gut. Now he just had to prove it to the stunad and his little pixie.

After checking his watch, he picked the microphone up from the table and announced, "Doms, you have fifteen minutes to impress Master Stefan with a design on your sub. And go!"

While the crowd's eyes were all on the competing Doms, Ian took great pleasure in watching Stefan watching Cain and Cassandra. The man would need a dentist soon if he didn't stop gritting his teeth so hard.

Over at the other end of the stage, Cain was making a mess of his ropes and not applying them to Cassie's wrists properly, which she held up in front of her chest while he worked. Although, if one looked closely, it was clear he'd left the rope loose enough not to hurt her. She was kneeling on the pillow, and from the expression on her face, she was holding back from telling the Dom he shouldn't be wrapping the rope around her wrists. Anyone who'd been trained in even the basics of Shibari knew to avoid the wrists where too tight a knot could damage the nerves there. The rope should be two inches higher or lower from any joint—in this case, higher on the arm.

Stefan crossed his arms and let out a low growl. "What the fuck is he doing?"

*Ha! This is too damn easy!*

Fighting back his laughter, Ian responded, "Guess he's going to lose points for that, isn't he?"

Over the next few minutes, Cain continued to "screw up." He left the ends of the rope dangling instead of tucking them safely into the design and tied knots the wrong way, where they would fall apart if Cassandra moved. The man looked around as if distracted by everything else going on, his focus not on his submissive as it should be.

When Cain brought a rope to Cassandra's neck and hesitated, Stefan stood up so fast, his chair would've gone flying off into the audience if Carter hadn't been standing to the side of the stage with quick reflexes. Every Dominant on the stage froze. With his eyebrows raised, Ian tilted his chin up to study Stefan. "Problem?"

The man's hands were balled into tight fists as he glowered at him. His voice was low and threatening, so only Ian and Mitch could hear him. "You son of a bitch. Foster's not this fucking stupid. You set this up."

Ian shrugged. "Maybe I did, maybe I didn't. Either way, it doesn't matter. What *does* matter is that the woman who's madly in love with you doesn't have your collar around her neck and is scening with another Dom. Why? Because you're either deaf, dumb, or blind, or a combination of all three. So, my question is, what the hell are you going to do about it?"

The other man's eyes had bulged when Ian had dropped the "L" word, and Mitch had noticed the reaction too. He laughed. "Why is it we guys are always the last to know when someone's in love with us?"

―――

*God damn, manipulative son of a bitch!* If Stefan thought he stood a chance against Sawyer, he'd kick his ass right then. But even when Stefan had been in the best shape of his life, the retired SEAL would've been a formidable opponent.

*And what the fuck is the guy talking about? Cassie's madly in love? With me?*

"You're crazy," he spat, but the man's words were tumbling through Stefan's mind. Was it possible she felt more for him than just as a friend or a Dom? Was that the reason why she'd asked him to remove her collar? Because she'd fallen in love with him, and he'd been oblivious to the fact? And what about how he felt? He'd been miserable after she'd failed to re-sign their contract. And the past few weeks, he'd really enjoyed getting to know her on more than just a superficial basis. But the icing on the cake was seeing her scene with another Dom. It wasn't just the fact that Foster was doing a craptastic job of fucking up the scene. It was the green-eyed monster raging within Stefan that told him Cassie meant more to him than any other woman ever had. He'd never wanted to rip another man's head off his shoulders like he did right then.

The realization hit Stefan like a sledgehammer—he was in love with his sweet, little pixie. He wanted her in his ropes, his bed, and his life. He wanted her to move in with him, so he could fall asleep next to her every night and wake up to her every morning. He wanted to help her study to become a nurse and then be the loudest one cheering when she was handed her diploma. He wanted all that and so much more... but only with Cassie.

Unable to take his eyes off her, he said, "I'm invoking my rights as the club's Shibari Master to stop their scene before he does something to hurt her."

While they all knew Foster would never do anything to purposely harm a submissive, it was the only reason Stefan could come up with for interfering with another Dom's scene with an uncollared sub. And if Stefan had his way, Cassie wouldn't be uncollared anymore after he sat down and had a long talk with her.

Ian stood. "I wholeheartedly agree the scene should be stopped. Playroom number fifteen is empty if you'd like to take the poor sub there and administer aftercare."

His eyes shifted sideways to glare at the man, but Ian held up his hand before Stefan could say anything. "Yeah, yeah,

yeah—I know. I'm a manipulative bastard, a prick, an asshole, and a son of a bitch all rolled into one—we've already established that—but at least I'm not a twat-knot. Go get your girl, Master Stefan, and make sure you don't screw it up this time."

He wasn't sure if he hadn't already screwed things up for good, but he knew if he didn't at least try to win Cassie back, he'd regret it for the rest of his life.

Striding across the stage, he was a man on a mission. Step one—stop the ridiculous scene. Step two—try not to take a swing at the retired Secret Service guy. Step three—stake his claim and take Cassie to the playroom. Step four—restrain her properly, and spill his guts, then hope she really did love him because, by God, he was in love with her.

"Master Cain, I assume you're in on Master Ian's little scheme. If that's the case, I won't demand you retake my class before letting you rope-play with another submissive. But as of right now, your scene is over." Damn, he'd said that calmer than he'd expected from himself at the moment.

Foster eyed him, then at something over Stefan's left shoulder. Glancing back, Stefan saw that Ian had followed him. The head Dom nodded at Foster, who smirked and dropped the rope he'd been holding. "Took you long enough—I was running out of ways to mess things up."

Stefan was fucking surrounded by manipulative bastards. Cassie hadn't truly been in any danger, but that wasn't the point. As the other man squatted and began to undo the poorly tied ropes around her wrists, upper torso, and thighs, Stefan interrupted him. "Stop. Cassie, eyes on me."

He knew she'd noticed him walking toward them, but like a good submissive, she'd kept her gaze on the floor before her. But she hadn't been good about everything. When she lifted her chin, and their eyes met, he crossed his arms and frowned at her. "What's your safeword?"

She blinked a few times before answering. "Um . . . red, Sir?"

"Are you asking me if that's your safeword, or are you telling me? And speak up."

A blush stained her cheeks at the reprimand in his tone. She cleared her throat, then spoke louder. "I'm sorry, Sir. My safeword is red."

"And if you needed to slow things down and discuss something that was worrying you, what would that safeword be?"

"Yellow, Sir."

A tic in his temple throbbed. His hand would make some serious contact with her ass in a little bit, but first things first. "You've been involved in rope play long enough to know what has the potential to hurt you and what doesn't, correct?"

"Y-yes, Sir."

"Then, explain to me why you didn't say your safeword when you realized what a shitty job Master Cain was doing with the ropes, especially when he tied them over your radial nerves."

She shook her head, her gaze zipping from his to Ian's and back again, as she started to realize she was in some serious trouble. "He—he wasn't hurting me, Sir. I-I didn't think . . ."

"Cassie, look at your wrists. Are the ropes in the proper position?"

Her eyes flittered to her arms, and she swallowed hard. "No, Sir, they aren't."

"Then why didn't you, at least, say your yellow safeword?"

Tears welled up in her eyes. "I-I . . . I don't know, Sir. I'm sorry."

"You'll be a lot sorrier in a little bit. You and I have things to discuss in private. For now, apologize to Master Cain for not saying your safewords, then inform him you won't be scening with him anymore tonight." She wouldn't be scening with Foster, or any other Dom, *ever* again if Stefan had his way, but she wasn't ready to hear that just yet.

Her brow furrowed in confusion. "Sir?"

"Don't make me repeat myself, little pixie. I'm very pissed off right now, and most of it is not directed at you. Don't change that."

Her eyes looked like saucers, but then she turned her head to peer up at Foster, who stepped closer to Ian so she didn't need to crane her neck. "I'm sorry I didn't say my safeword, Master Cain. I knew what you were doing was wrong, and even though I didn't think you would hurt me, I still should have, at least, said, 'yellow,' and asked why you were wrapping the ropes directly over my wrists."

"Yes, you should have, Cassandra, but since this was all a ploy to get Stefan to man up, I'll forgive you."

Her face scrunched up, confirming to Stefan she had no idea what the Doms had been up to. "Man up, Sir? I don't understand."

"I'll explain later, Cassie," Stefan assured her. "You still need to say one more thing to Master Cain."

"Yes, Sir." She focused on the other Dom again. "I'm sorry, Sir, but I won't be finishing the scene with you. I'm also sorry if that means you can't compete for the free month of club fees."

Foster grinned. "No worries, little one. I wasn't expecting you to. And don't worry about the prize. Master Ian has already taken care of that."

*Of course, he has. Fucking manipulative . . . sigh. I can't keep calling him a bastard because that insults Marie and Chuck Sawyer, who are really nice people. They can't help it if their grown son is an asshole.*

*Well, enough about Ian. You've got more important things to take care of.*

Stefan took a step forward and went down on one knee. It

only took a few moments to release Cassie from the ropes, and he dropped them on the floor. Standing, he held out his hand to her and helped her to her feet. "Ian, you and Mitch will have to judge the rest of the contest yourselves—although, I'm sure you already knew that. Come, little pixie, you and I have some things to discuss."

A flash of panic appeared on her face, but it was gone just as quickly as it'd come. Stefan's gut churned. Was Ian wrong about Cassie loving him? God, he hoped that wasn't the case—not after Stefan had finally realized he was in love with her.

Bending forward, he put his shoulder into her abdomen and gently threw her over his shoulder, caveman style. Yeah, Dewayne would probably yell at him for overexerting himself—not that Cassie weighed all that much—but it was time for Stefan to stake his claim, and no one was going to stop him.

# Twenty-Two

Cass let out a short shriek as she was unexpectedly thrown over Stefan's shoulder, and his hand came down hard on her ass, eliciting a less audible squeak. "Quiet, little pixie."

He quickly descended the few steps from the stage to the pit floor, then strode purposely toward the playrooms. Cass was beyond confused, and it had all started when Master Ian called her that morning to ask if she was free tonight. When she'd told him her class had been canceled due to a death in her professor's family, he'd demanded her presence at the club promptly at 7:00 p.m., dressed in her favorite corset set.

When she arrived at The Covenant and was advised she would be scening with Master Cain for a contest, she'd almost wished she did have a class to be at. Not that she didn't like Master Cain, but she hadn't scened with anyone since her collar had been removed. Then, when Master Stefan had shown up and walked down the grand staircase, Cass had wished the floor would open up and swallow her whole. She was still mad at him and distressed about everything that had happened over the last few months. Seeing him tonight had just made those emotions blaze hotter. But instead of saying her safeword, she'd obeyed Master Ian's order to be a submissive for the event.

Hanging down Stefan's back, Cass bounced and swayed with every step he took but knew he wouldn't drop her. She was, however, worried about him exerting himself. "Master Stefan, please put me—"

He lit up her ass cheek again. His voice was low and threatening. "I said to be quiet, Cassie. Keep it up, and I'll gag you."

Okay, so he was *really* pissed off, but so was she. Unfortunately, here at the club, she had to be respectful to any and all Doms or face public punishment.

Entering what she assumed was Playroom #15—it was hard to tell, at first, since she was upside down, facing Stefan's muscular back and ass—he slammed the door shut. Her upper body was flipped back over his shoulder so quickly her head spun, and she was dropped unceremoniously onto a bed with clean, burgundy sheets. She bounced on the mattress, then settled as Stefan pivoted and stalked back and forth.

He pointed but didn't look at her as he moved. "Not a word out of you until I get my anger under control, Cassie. Again, most of it isn't directed at you, but since you're the only one here at the moment, you're the only one I can potentially take it out on, so just sit there and be quiet for a few minutes."

*Okaaayyy.* Cass had never seen him this mad before, and her own anger ebbed a bit and morphed into a combination of worry and bewilderment. Had she ruined things between them by going off on him yesterday and then scening with Master Cain tonight? Not that things had been all that great between them to begin with. She was totally in love with the man, and to him, she was nothing more than a friend and submissive who enjoyed his ropes. But if that was the case, why was he so pissed off?

Thinking back to what'd happened on the center stage, she recalled Master Cain saying something about it all being some sort of "a ploy to get Stefan to man up." What the hell had he been talking about? And what about that knowing smirk she'd seen on Master Ian's face? The Dom had definitely been up to something.

Stopping short, Stefan ran his hands down his face and huffed. Then he shocked her when he dropped to his knees at the foot of the bed, grabbed her ankles, and pulled her until she sat on the edge. Taking her hands in his, he stared at her with a look she'd never seen in his eyes before. If she had to give it a name, it would be anguish. "Little pixie, I screwed up. I really screwed up, and I'm so, so sorry."

Now she was really confused. "What are you talking about, Sir?"

He kissed her fingers. "I should never have let you go. When you asked me to uncollar you, I should've fought harder to find out why you didn't want to renew our contract. With everything that's happened over the past few weeks, I've had my ups and downs, but you've been there every step of the way for me. Whether I wanted you to be there or not. Like a fool, I've denied my feelings for you."

He took a deep breath, blew it out, and stared her right in the eye. "Somewhere along the line, little pixie, I've done something I swore I'd never do—because I suck at relationships—but I've fallen in love with you."

Cassie gasped but didn't interrupt Stefan as he continued talking. Her heart was ready to beat out of her chest, and she wished he would repeat what he'd just said, so she could make sure she hadn't misheard him.

"As I said, I've never been good at relationships—had a

few bad ones in my twenties—so, since then, I've always had short-term contracts with subs. I knew with an expiration date, I didn't have to worry about my heart getting involved. But none of those subs lasted as long as you have, and now I know why. You're special, Cassie, and I don't want to let you go. Tell me why you didn't want to renew our contract because I don't think you told me the whole truth that night."

Her body shook. She never thought she'd be saying those three little words to him, but before she did, she had to be certain. "Can you go back a few seconds, first, and repeat what I think you said? What I hope you said."

The corners of his mouth ticked upward, and he tilted his head. "The part about me sucking at relationships or the part where I said I've fallen in love with you?"

Cassie nodded. "Definitely the second part."

Rising on his knees, he cupped her jaw and brushed his lips against hers in the sweetest of all kisses. "I love you, little pixie, and if I have my way, I'll be the only Dom you ever play with again. Now, tell me what I want to know."

Tears welled up in her eyes, but they were happy ones this time. Reaching up, she stroked his clean-shaven cheek. She couldn't speak louder than a whisper as she was still afraid this was all a dream. "I didn't exactly lie to you, but you're right. I only told you part of the reason why I didn't want to re-sign the contract. I just couldn't stay in a strictly D/s relationship with you because I'd fallen in love with you too."

Relief flashed in his eyes, and she realized he'd been worried about her response. "Thank God."

His mouth crashed down on hers. After a moment of shock, she parted her lips and let their tongues tango. Her arms went around his neck, and she opened her legs further, encouraging him to close the distance between them.

God, she'd missed his taste.

His scent.

His warmth.

His strength.

Him.

Leaving her mouth, he kissed his way along her jawline to her ear. "I love you, Cassie." He pulled back, and his gaze roamed her face. His eyes pleaded with her as much as his words did. "Please say you forgive me for not seeing what was right in front of me all these months. For being an ass yesterday. For not giving a crap what happened to me because I was foolish to think there was nothing else in my life but the Coast Guard. Please tell me it's not too late to show you how much you mean to me."

"It's not, Sir. And there's nothing to forgive as long as you're here with me now. Just tell me you'll come back to rehab and do everything you can to be around for a very long time. I don't want to lose you."

His thumbs brushed over her cheeks, wiping away the tears she didn't realize had started to fall. All she could do was hope she wasn't dreaming.

"I don't want to lose you either, Cassie. You're mine. It just took me getting a swift kick in the ass, or the chest, as the case may be, to realize that. You'll never play with another Dom again as long as I'm alive, and I plan on being around to love you for a very long time. I'll go back to rehab, I'll eat nutritiously, and I'll take my meds. I'll do everything you tell me to do when it comes to getting better and staying healthy. In return, you submit to me. You'll wear my collar, and any contract we sign won't have an expiration date. Okay?"

She nodded as best she could with her head still in his hands. "That's more than okay, Sir."

---

Letting go of her jaw, Stefan turned his attention to her corset. "Now that we've settled all that, I'm going to strip you naked and make love to you. Tonight, it's just you and me. No audience. No ropes. No restraints. No toys. I'll give you pleasure, and you'll give me your orgasms."

A worried look flashed across her face, and he stopped unlacing the corset. "What's wrong? Are you afraid I won't be able to get you off without restraints?"

When her eyes rounded, he knew he'd been right on the mark. "Trust me, little pixie. I'll take care of you. I'll make you come and scream my name. You don't need to be tied down—you just need my love."

He saw the moment his words and their meaning penetrated her mind.

Her eyes were filled with desire.

With hope.

With submission.

With undying love.

Stefan returned to her corset and the rest of her outfit, and it wasn't long before she was completely naked. Standing, he quickly shed his clothing. Before doing anything else, he stepped over to a cabinet and retrieved a handful of condoms. Once he started making love to her, he didn't want there to be any excuse to leave her, even for a second. After tossing the foil packages onto a small table beside the bed, he knelt in front of her again. "Lie back, pixie."

Once she complied, he put his hands behind her thighs and pushed them up until her knees were almost against her chest. He took a moment to enjoy the view. Cassie had such a pretty, hairless pussy. One that made his mouth water. Juices were already making her slit glisten, and he bent down for a taste.

Cassie gasped loudly as he ran his tongue up through her folds. Her back bowed when he sucked on her clit, drawing a moan of pleasure from her. Her scent and taste were intoxicating as he nipped, licked, and sucked on her intimate flesh. He loved how she squirmed and ran her fingers through his hair, which had been growing out since his heart attack. Cassie rarely got her hands on him during play. She'd always been restrained in some way or another. After she'd come more than once, he'd used her mouth, pussy, or ass to find his own release. But tonight, he wanted her touching him—all over—learning every inch of his body as much as he'd learned hers during their many scenes together.

When he flicked her clit rapidly with his tongue, Cassie dug her nails into his shoulders, and the erotic pain spurred him on. Reaching up with one hand, he tweaked her nipple. With a squeak, her hips bucked, and there was a rush of fluid that he lapped up. Stefan knew Cassie had never come without restraints before, and he wanted to change that. She was such a sensual creature, and with the right Dom—the right man—she should be able to fly.

As he continued to tease her breast and suck her clit, he slid one, then two, fingers inside her, finding her walls already quivering with anticipation. He fucked her slowly as her moans and writhing increased. When she began to beg for release, it was music to his ears. "No protocol, my pixie. Come whenever you need to."

She lifted her hips in invitation. "I need . . . oh my God, Sir! I need . . ." She panted, then gasped. "More! Almost . . . there! Pleeeeeeease!"

Using his tongue, he lashed at her clit while increasing the thrusting of his fingers inside her. He rolled her nipple between his thumb and forefinger, then pinched it hard at the same time he bit down on her clit.

Cassie exploded into space. She screamed as the climax gripped her, infusing her with such intense pleasure she squirted all over his fingers. But Stefan wasn't satisfied with just one orgasm from her. He pulled on her nipple, torturing the little peak, while rubbing her inside where he knew her G-spot was. Lifting his head slightly, he blew on her abused clit, and Cassie screeched that time as her body shook uncontrollably.

Stefan drew out the orgasm as long as he could until Cassie sagged against the mattress, completely spent and sated. Her skin was covered in perspiration, and he licked the saltiness from her abdomen.

Climbing up onto the bed, he dragged her further into the middle, then grabbed a condom from the stash. As he rolled it on his aching cock, he smiled when he saw her watching him through half-lidded eyes. When she licked her lips, he groaned. "As much as I would love to see your lips around my cock, pixie, I'd prefer to be inside your sweet pussy this time.

After settling between her widespread thighs, he held himself at her entrance. Before he took her, he had to say it again. "I love you, Cassie. You're mine."

"Yours, Sir," she responded with a sigh. "Only yours. Always."

He pushed inside her, relishing her wet heat sheathing him. His eyes slammed shut as he tried to stave off his impending orgasm. When he was balls deep, Cassie lifted her legs and wrapped them around his hips. He felt her heels on his ass, spurring him on. Withdrawing, he plunged back in. Then again. And again. He fucked her with abandon, feeling a connection he'd never had with another sub or any woman for that matter. She was his, and he was branding her . . . ruining her for any other man.

A tingling sensation began in his spine. Sweat poured from his body, slicking wherever their skin touched. Cassie's begging and keening began again, and her walls shuddered around him. Reaching between them, he found her clit and pushed down on it. That sent her over the edge, dragging him with her into a seemingly bottomless pit of pleasure and euphoria.

Struggling for air, Stefan gave her some of his weight without crushing her or restricting her own search for oxygen. He touched his soaked forehead to hers. "I love you, my pixie. I'll always love you."

# Epilogue

"Stefan!" Elin squealed when she spotted him from across the hotel lobby in Key West, Florida. His sister ran into his arms and hugged him tightly as her fiancée joined them.

"Hey, sis." He squeezed her, then let go. Turning to Tara, he embraced her as well. "Hey, sister-in-law-to-be. How're you doing?"

"I'm excited, thrilled, and ready to party, all rolled into one."

Stefan chuckled as he released her. "Sounds like you're all set to go." Pivoting, he reached behind him. "C'mere, little pixie." Cassie put her hand in his and stepped forward. "Elin, Tara, this is Cassie."

She beamed and gave Elin a hug and then Tara. "It's so nice to meet you finally. I feel like we already met after Skyping the past three months."

Stefan had introduced them over the internet and ensured Cassie was at the townhouse with him at least once a week when he checked in with his sister and Tara. He'd wanted them all to get to know each other because he planned on proposing to Cassie in a few weeks. His sister had tried to talk him into doing the deed this weekend, but he hadn't wanted to steal Elin and Tara's thunder. This was their weekend, and Stefan and Cassie's time would come another day.

It wasn't as if they weren't already headed in that direction. Two weeks after Stefan had groveled and won Cassie's heart and forgiveness, he'd officially collared her in a large ceremony on the center stage at The Covenant. Afterward, he'd decorated her in the angel Shibari design he'd wanted to do with her the night she'd said her safeword and failed to renew their contract.

The following weekend, their friends helped her move into his townhouse. It was so nice for Stefan to go home after a full day at the Trident Security compound, where he was already fully engrossed in his new career, to find Cassie waiting for him. If it were a school night for her, he'd cook dinner or bring home takeout—healthy takeout—and on the other nights, they'd prepare their evening meal together. Afterward, they either cuddled while watching TV, went to a movie, took walks around the neighborhood, and did all other kinds of things couples did. Oh, and of course, they played and made love often. They'd fall asleep in each other's arms, then wake up the same way. The routine had become so comfortable that Stefan often wondered why he'd been fighting a deeper relationship with her for as long as he had.

"It's great to finally meet you, too, and we're so glad you could come for the wedding," Elin responded.

After a few weeks of back and forth, trying to decide where and when they wanted to get married, the engaged couple chose that weekend in the Florida Keys. Tomorrow, about forty family and friends would gather for the nuptials and the after-party. The women wanted an unostentatious affair, so they would exchange vows on the beach. Then everyone would join them for a buffet dinner and drinks at the

Mango Tree Inn near Duvall Street in Old Town Key West, which was within walking distance of the hotel.

"Thanks for inviting me. It's been ages since I've been to Key West. I've been watching The Weather Channel all week, and it's supposed to be gorgeous this weekend. Perfect timing."

"Where are Mom and Dad?" Stefan asked, glancing around the lobby.

"They walked across the street to get us a table for lunch after you texted you were leaving the airport," Tara responded. "It's just the six of us for now. Everyone else is on their own until tonight when we're all meeting up at Sunset Pier for dinner and drinks."

"Great." Stefan flagged over a man at the concierge desk, wearing khaki shorts and a polo shirt with the hotel's name and logo on it. "Can you hold our luggage for a bit? Then we'll check in after lunch."

"Absolutely, sir. Let me get you a claim ticket."

Five minutes later, they joined Stefan's folks in the restaurant, where there was another round of greetings and hugs. His mother was thrilled to see Cassie again, and it made Stefan happy to know his parents really liked her.

Being the gentleman he'd been raised to be, Stefan pulled out a chair for his little pixie, then took the seat next to her.

"How was the flight?" his father asked him after a waitress took their drink orders.

"Fantastic."

Cassie's mouth dropped open as she stared at his amused grin. "What are you talking about? That turbulence was so bad at one point I had a death grip on you. I wanted to climb into your lap and get under *your* seat belt."

"Like I said, it was fantastic."

Everyone else laughed as she slapped his upper arm indignantly. Her cheeks were bright red, her embarrassment showing for a few moments before she giggled. "Jerk."

God, he loved her. She was the best thing that'd ever happened to him, and he was never taking her for granted ever again. Reaching over, he tweaked her nose. "Pixie."

Her smile and the adoration in her eyes warmed his heart —the one that had given him a second chance at life and love.

The server brought their drinks, and Stefan waited until everyone had theirs. He picked up his glass and said, "I'd like to propose a toast. To family, love, and new beginnings. Cheers."

"Cheers!"

---

If you're following the best reading order of the Trident Security series and its spinoff series, *Blood Bound: Blackhawk Security Book 2* is next on the list!

Also by

***Denotes titles/series that are available on select digital sites only. Paperbacks and audiobooks are available on most book sites.

## THE TRIDENT SECURITY SERIES

*Leather & Lace*

*His Angel*

*Waiting For Him*

*Not Negotiable: A Novella*

*Topping The Alpha*

*Watching From the Shadows*

*Whiskey Tribute: A Novella*

*Tickle His Fancy*

*No Way in Hell: A Steel Corp/Trident Security Crossover (co-authored with J.B. Havens)*

*Absolving His Sins*

*Option Number Three: A Novella*

*Salvaging His Soul*

*Trident Security Field Manual*

*Torn In Half: A Novella*

### ***Heels, Rhymes, & Nursery Crimes Series
#### (with 13 other authors)

*Jack Be Nimble: A Trident Security-Related Short Story*

### ***The Deimos Series

*Handling Haven: Special Forces: Operation Alpha*
*Cheating the Devil: Special Forces: Operation Alpha*

### The Trident Security Omega Team Series

*Mountain of Evil*
*A Dead Man's Pulse*
*Forty Days & One Knight*

### The Doms of The Covenant Series

*Double Down & Dirty*
*Entertaining Distraction*
*Knot a Chance*

### The Blackhawk Security Series

*Tuff Enough*
*Blood Bound*

### Master Key Series

*Master Key Resort*
*Master Cordell*

### Hazard Falls Series

*Don't Fight It*
*Don't Shoot the Messenger*

### THE MALONE BROTHERS SERIES

*Take the Money and Run*

*The Devil's Spare Change*

### LARGO RIDGE SERIES

*Cold Feet*

### ANTELOPE ROCK SERIES
### (CO-AUTHORED WITH J.B. HAVENS)

*Wannabe in Wyoming*

*Wistful in Wyoming*

### AWARD-WINNING STANDALONE BOOKS

*The Road to Solace*

*Scattered Moments in Time: A Collection of Short Stories & More*

### ***THE BID ON LOVE SERIES
### (WITH 7 OTHER AUTHORS!)

*Going, Going, Gone: Book 2*

### ***THE COLLECTIVE: SEASON TWO
### (WITH 7 OTHER AUTHORS!)

*Angst: Book 7*

### SPECIAL COLLECTIONS

*Trident Security Series: Volume I*

*Trident Security Series: Volume II*

*Trident Security Series: Volume III*

*Trident Security Series: Volume IV*

*Trident Security Series: Volume V*

*Trident Security Series: Volume VI*

About

*USA Today* Bestselling Author and Award-Winning Author Samantha Cole is a retired policewoman and former paramedic. Using her life experiences and training, she strives to find the perfect mix of suspense and romance for her readers to enjoy.

Awards:

*Wannabe in Wyoming* (co-authored by J.B. Havens) won the bronze medal in the 2021 Readers' Favorite Awards in the General Romance category.

*Scattered Moments in Time*, won the gold medal in the 2020 Readers' Favorite Awards in the Fiction Anthology category.

*The Road to Solace* (formerly *The Friar*), won the silver medal in the 2017 Readers' Favorite Awards in the Contemporary Romance category.

Samantha has over thirty-five books published throughout several different series as well as a few standalone novels. A full list can be found on her website.

Sexy Six-Pack's Sirens Group on Facebook
Website: www.samanthacoleauthor.com
Newsletter: www.geni.us/SCNews

- facebook.com/SamanthaColeAuthor
- instagram.com/samanthacoleauthor
- bookbub.com/profile/samantha-a-cole
- goodreads.com/SamanthaCole
- tiktok.com/@samanthacoleauthor